G000060974

Optimist's
Apprentice

The Optimist's Apprentice

Will two strong personalities from different walks of life create success or chaos . . .

WILLIAM TELLS

THE CLOISTER HOUSE PRESS

Copyright © 2023 William Tells

All rights reserved. No part of this publication may be
reproduced or transmitted in any form or by any means,
electronic or mechanical including photocopying, recording or
any information storage or retrieval system, without prior
permission in writing from the publishers.

The right of William Tells to be identified as the author of this
work has been asserted by him in accordance with the Copyright,
Designs and Patents Act 1988

First published in the United Kingdom in 2023 by
The Cloister House Press

ISBN 978-1-913460-62-4

Dedication

꩜

My Father was a free spirit, a lover of life and ever the optimist.

On 13th February 1994 at 47 years old, he suffered a major stroke which affected the right side of his body and the doctors told us to prepare to say goodbye as he only had one month to live.

Well, it was almost 29 years later on 1st January 2023 that he finally decided it was time to leave this world.

He was determined to experience as much as he could and live a lot longer than any doctor dictated he should. Also he had to live long enough to write this story of course, which he said just rolled into his head and kept him entertained during lockdown 2020 (despite only having one able – and not even his best – writing hand to do so).

Whilst clearing out his things I found a few more unpublished manuscripts written before and after his stroke which I am eager to read through. Amongst these was a little green post it note onto which he had hand written the following words, which I think shed a little more light on the kind of man William was:

My Epitaph

꥟

Strong as an ox
Stubborn as an old mule
And I loved every day of my life
Both the good days and the bad days

I also found what I think may have formed part of what he would have written as his foreword:

This isn't a love story, at least I don't think so.

It's all about taking a chance to improve your goal in life, but you must listen to your gut instinct before you say yes.

If someone offers you the chance of a lifetime, give it a little thought and then grab it with both hands.

The path you will take in your lifetime is completely unknown, you just have to sort it out day by day!

So the story of 'The Optimist's Apprentice' is now a part of his creative legacy that he has gifted to those who choose to read it.

Over the years of us sharing time on this Earth together he has increasingly inspired me to create without fear and I expect he will continue to inspire me in spirit too.

Chapter One

Old smoggy London Town was not a healthy living place in the 1860s, but a young kid aged thirteen still had to make a living on the streets and Shiner was one of them.

He did rather well for himself because he had two means of making some pennies at the same spot, just off Liverpool Street quite near the railway station.

He had a contract selling newspapers, for which he had to go to Fleet Street every morning to pick up a batch at six in the morning. He had made a little trolley out of wood just for that purpose. This trolley had another purpose: it could be converted into a shoeshine seat and a little step to rest your feet on, ready to shine on anyone who needed a fine polish on their footwear. For this task, he would charge you the princely sum of one penny and also persuade you to buy a paper to read whilst he covered your footwear in a fine shine.

He always would wear a grey greatcoat while he was working, come rain or come sunshine, because this coat belonged to his dearly departed dad and it made him feel cosy, warm and safe. His mum passed away soon after his dad and so therefore he was existing on the streets of London as an orphan. However, he had high hopes for better things in his short life because he was a born optimist and willing to try anything – except stealing from other people, because although he had little money, he was brought up with strong morals.

Halfway through this particular day he was just about ready to eat his pork pie and swig into his beer when he got a tap on the shoulder and there stood his next customer. He observed it was an elderly gent very well dressed and he needed a little shine on his perfectly clean shoes, so he sat down on the seat provided after the boy gave it a little wipe and handed him a copy of the latest edition of today's news. So once again lunch can wait because every penny counts.

This old boy also carried a large leather bag which seemed rather heavy and he placed this beside the chair and after the boy finished the shine and stood back, the old gent got up tucked the paper under his arm, paid the boy a few pennies and left quickly without the said bag. The boy shouted after him, 'Hey, mister, you have forgotten your bag!' and he ran after him, but he had disappeared into the crowd and then the boy realised it wouldn't be safe to leave his stand vacant for too long in this part of the city.

So then he sat down and had his much-needed lunch and counted his takings today, but that big leather bag was playing on his brain. He decided to have a look inside and he picked it up and said to himself, 'God that is heavy, no wonder he left it here.' Now he was curious at the contents so he snapped open the top catch but along came his next client, so he then snapped the catch shut again.

So it was back to work as usual, must earn some

2

money, no time to sit about. But that day he had sold all of his papers just before four o'clock leaving him some free time to examine the contents. Right at the top of the inside there was an address and the name of the company. But what was in it? A whole load of little round glasses, some bits of bent wire that looked like spider legs and a whole load of papers with strange symbols which only an expert, in whatever language this was, could read and he said to himself, 'Now let's get this back to the old gent.'

He checked the address one more time and remarked, 'This is only a few streets away,' and so off he went into the big posh offices. There was a lady at the reception desk, and after she positioned her glasses at the end of her nose and gave him a real filthy look she asked him, 'Well, scruffy boy, what do you want?' and he retorted without a quiver, 'Well, missus, I must see Mr Scarlet. I have his bag, can I see him?' Then she stood up, pushed her glasses back in position and replied, 'Certainly not! So why do you have his bag?' to which he explained politely, 'I am the shoeshine boy and he left it beside my chair but forgot to pick it up when he left,' and she retorted, 'Ah thank goodness, that bag. Let me call him down, he thought finding it was a lost cause and that you would have sold it already.' The boy calmly replied, 'Not me. That is close to stealing in my book.'

Then in came Mr Scarlet with a beaming smile on his face and said to the young lad, 'Now you have redeemed my faith in human nature. What a treasure to find a lad with an honest outlook in life. So what is your name?' and he replied, 'Most people on the street call me Shiner, but my true name is William and I don't know my surname. Is that okay?' And the old gent remarked, 'Fine by me,' and added, 'Thank you for returning my bag. So, you can read? Did you go to school? How old are you?' and he reluctantly replied, 'Just going on fourteen, why?' Now, not many people took much of an interest in his past, and he was a bit wary of all these questions and thought "I have done nothing wrong, just give me the bloody tip and I will leave." But that wasn't going to happen because this old gent took quite a shine to this young street lad for his downright honest approach to his life and he sussed out that he was keen to leave. He asked him straight out, 'So what did you think about the contents of the bag?' and the boy replied, 'Strangely quite interesting. They look like eyeglasses but not quite finished yet. So where is my tip?'

Mr Scarlet just loved his forthright approach and said, 'Is two shillings enough for your time?' and he replied, 'It is a bloody fortune, thanks, mister,' and he then turned towards the doorway when he grasped the coin in his hand. But then the old gent called after him, 'Would you like to work in my workshop to learn the trade? I will pay you well.' Now this the boy didn't expect and he turned and replied, 'I have only four years of schooling. Is that enough?' and the old gent remarked, 'That is enough for me. You have the right attitude to get on and probably more than most in these times,' and the boy replied, 'Okay I will take it, thanks, but give me a week to transfer my present business to one of my good friends on the street.'

Mr Scarlet called to him, 'Fine, that suits me, see

you a week Monday at eight in the morning prompt,' and added, 'Have a good wash before you come. We will supply you with an overall, and good luck for next week.' William couldn't believe his luck that he was about to gain a proper trade, in a proper business to further his life in the big city.

Now this was not in his plan for life, but he took the opportunity because it was a break from the humdrum life he was living now. He had to transfer his shoe cleaning and paper stand to someone he could fully trust and, to him, there was only one person who would do. That was young James, who was new to the street but an honest and sensible lad just like himself. He invited him down to his pitch to see what he could do and he tried him out with a few clients of his and then he went down to the local pawn shop to purchase some new clothes for his new job. The following Monday he arrived outside the optician's door, took a deep breath and pushed open the highly polished door. The lady on reception actually gave him a smile and told him, 'Go straight upstairs, he is waiting for you,' and then he sighed with relief and realised he was not dreaming. "I am truly in and up." He walked into the workshop and then he saw a row of men all busy on their benches and Mr Scarlet put out his hand and said, 'Welcome to the firm, young William, you cleaned up pretty well. Here is your bench. Fred will show you the basics of the process of assembling and he will even teach you how to do eye testing on people, but don't rush yourself, just take it step by step.' He then asked, 'So where do you live?' William hesitated slightly and admitted he lived on the street and the old gent said, 'That would never do whilst you're working in here.' Then he paused slightly and suggested, 'We have got an old attic room not in use. You can sleep up there, but there is a catch, the shop is locked up at six in the evening so anything you need has to be brought in before lock in.' William replied gratefully, 'Fine by me.' He then had a quick look round the workshop and was quite amazed by all the instruments on the benches and wondered if he would ever manage to fit in here.

It took some time and hard work on his part but finally, three years later, he passed his degree and became a fully qualified optometrist at the fine old age of seventeen and was therefore entitled to earn a bit more salary to add to his ever growing bank account, which the old gent set up for him at the beginning of his employment. But he wasn't quite a rich young man yet; that would come later in his life, with a bit more hard work and a little more thought.

On a sunny afternoon one day in May, Mr Scarlet called down Fred from the workshop and asked him, 'What do you think about this new land of America and especially New York? According to The Times newspaper it is thriving beyond most and I think it is a good idea to start up a shop there. Are you game to go there?' He answered, 'Well I might think about it but I will need a small team, maybe of two. I will take Tim and maybe young William if that is okay?' and Mr Scarlet remarked, 'A good choice. Both are hard-working and fit and I will give you a budget of two thousand pounds for the whole project. I have already booked an agent for some property in the town but make sure you haggle for the best price for everything and give it your best to succeed over there and good luck.'

Then Fred had to persuade the two chosen ones and that was pretty easy. Tim jumped at the chance for a new life in a new town abroad because his life was pretty boring in London Town and young William said, 'Let me think about it. How long would we be at sea?' and he answered, 'About fourteen or fifteen days.' William replied, 'I have never been at sea before,' and Fred remarked, 'Neither have I. Just let it roll. Lots of people have been before. You are a young lad so it will be a piece of cake for you!' Then he answered confidently, 'Okay I am up for it so when do we leave?'

Fred replied, 'Don't know yet, it is up to the old man to book the sailing and prepare all of the paperwork and arrange some properties for us to view and I think it would be pretty soon, so don't go making any plans for a short holiday right now!' He replied, 'I won't, so will we have to take some of our stock there to start trading?' Fred remarked, 'Pretty much all of our tools and glasses and wire. We will need one very big box to carry that lot, but I suppose he had worked that out before he even mentioned the plan to me. He is one real sharp pencil.' Young William then enquired, 'So just how far is it on the ship?' and he replied, 'about three thousand miles. I think it is a pretty big pond!'

Chapter Two

⌐≈⌐

The day of sailing arrived just two weeks later and they loaded their big crate into the hold and took their places in the cabin. But this was no luxury liner which didn't surprise them because they all knew that the old gent was very canny with his money but they really didn't mind that.

The voyage was a good mix of rough and not so smooth but they got there after fourteen days at sea because it was a transport cargo ship and was built for speed in all weathers. When they actually sailed into the harbour, they all gave a mighty cheer along with the crew but now they had to be quite aware of walking on dry land again so they carefully trod on the concrete landing entrance into the port, slowly slowly, just to get their feet accustomed once more. Fred took care of their cargo with one of the dockhands to put it in storage for some time until they had acquired a suitable property for the firm and now they were all ready for a bite to eat and a beer.

William then asked one of the men where the nearest cafe was and he pointed out, 'This is the main entrance and there is the main road; you will see it there just on the left' and added, 'New in town? I see you came in on the old steamer. How did you find it?' William remarked, 'Not too bad, my first time on the sea and maybe my last!' and the man replied, 'A wise answer. I did exactly the same trip about three years ago.'

Now they were heading for the real estate agent's on Bleecker Street and it was only within walking distance, so they decided to saunter there to think over how to approach the agent. In they went to pick up the keys to the said property and a young assistant said to them, 'I will show you around the property if you like. It is no trouble to me, all part of the service,' and Fred replied, 'Fine suits me, I love to have a good look around with someone who has the knowledge of the said subject.' They gave the property a good viewing. Then Fred asked her that vital question which was, 'So how much is he asking?' The young lady told him and William then butted in, 'It is much too much. The whole front has to be redone and the inside looks like a tip! And also the floor is rotting in some places! I will offer him half the asking price and I will give you a fifty-dollar bill if you can seal the deal in cash,' and the lady said, 'Okay I will put your offer to him today.' This young lady knew this young fellow was not quite as he seems and was a true negotiator, not just some ordinary Joe off the street and she did so. His offer was accepted that same day and he presented her with a crisp fifty-dollar bill just as he promised when she handed the keys over to him along with the money for the shop's deeds.

So they moved into their new shop and it was a real tip but no real problem for them because all three of them were used to a bit of hard work and they swept the place clean and repainted the walls. But for the rest of the work they hired proper people to lay out their plans for a new shop along with new desks, a big front window complete with gold lettering and a big fat strong door. Then it was down to business. The first few months were a touch slow because they were not really public people and then William had an idea to hire a lady to man the desk at the entrance. She was a former client, but one clever straightforward lady with a polite voice, well-dressed, had a local family and said 'Yes' to the offer. William was truly delighted; her name was Roseanne and she was happy to make some extra money for her family.

After that the clients just rolled in and all three of them were busy on eye testing at least half of their day and the other was spent up in their workshop. Then they slept up in the attic room on three mattresses, which they bought in a second-hand store along with six old blankets and some pillows which they bought new along with some sheets. Yes, it was a bit rough at first but they were on a real tight budget. Did they care? Well not really, the shop was now paying its way and every week some new clients appeared due to their reputation for their quick turnover and of course their reasonable prices. Then Fred asked his young new former apprentice quietly, 'Now you, young man, have a talent for acquiring pretty young ladies. We need one more girl in the shop for sales so go out there and find one,' but William asked him, 'So why me? I know nothing about them!' and Fred replied, 'That is exactly why you are so appealing to them, so go look for one and make sure it is a real pretty one.' The sun was shining, the day was hot with just a tiny breeze and there were lots of people around. Then

Fred gave him some cash for a butty and a coffee for him and Tim to eat in the shop and out he went on his mission to pick up a young shop girl.

It was almost lunchtime and so he popped into their local cafe just around the corner and it was almost full. Then he spotted a vacant seat and asked the young lady sitting there, 'Young miss do you mind if I sit here?' and she looked up and replied, 'Help yourself,' and added, 'Are you new in town?' He responded, 'No not really, me and my fellow workers run a shop just around the corner but we are very busy and so we don't really get out much. So what is your name?' and she replied, 'Nicole,' and he remarked, 'Nice name. What do you do?' and she quickly replied, 'Oh I do everything. So what do you fancy?' He then remarked with a little smile, 'I would like a new girl in my shop and you might just be the one,' and added, 'Meet me tomorrow in here at 1.15 but wash that muck off of your face and dress properly, because my big boss is pretty proper,' and added, 'Can you read and write and count?' 'Absolutely,' she replied, 'I am very good at it. I have been at school for seven years!' and he remarked, 'That will do very nicely so see you then.' Then she enquired, 'So why pick me?' and he replied, 'It's just like an old man's intuition, that is all, so be there prompt,' and she said, 'I will but you will have to buy the coffee. I am out of funds,' and he then remarked, 'No problem.' She then arrived at the shop the following day just after lunch and Fred gave her a good look over and said to William, 'She will do, you have a fine talent there, don't lose it,' and William told

Nicole, 'You are in. Fred will sort out your salary,' and she excitedly exclaimed, 'That was real easy!' Then Fred remarked to her, 'You have to know the right people and that young man is one of them,' and William then went out and wired Mr Scarlet the good news and he was pretty pleased of his young protégé's progress because he knew he had picked a winner from the very start.

Now William felt he was free to embark on what he really intended which was to sell their glasses to the big wide open countryside in the big plains of America even though he knew nothing about that area, but that didn't put him off. He put an advertisement in a magazine which would circulate around all of the trading posts and forts in the west and he put his own money into it and then he approached Fred with his idea who remarked, 'It is simply madness. How will you get there? It is full of native Indians and wild cowboys!' 'I have no fear for either of them,' he replied 'I will travel by a wagon to reach them and I will make the wagon really visible,' and Fred remarked, 'You are truly mad!' But that comment didn't put him off and so he set his sights on the wild west and asked Fred for six weeks off with no pay. Fred agreed with that and wished him good luck and William just gave him an ironic smile back and said, 'It is good for our shop!'

Now he was on the lookout for a suitable wagon and he tried several farms nearby but there was no luck there and then he was walking back to the shop and passing their local police station. He spotted the perfect vehicle parked just outside with a big paper notice stating, 'This wagon is for sale please enquire at the desk inside.' But there was no price on it and that triggered his street instinct that it was going to be real cheap and so in he went and asked the desk sergeant straight out. He asked him flatly, 'How much? I have got the cash on me now.' The desk sergeant replied, 'Well really we were thinking about twenty dollars.' William shook his head and stated, 'That is not going to happen. I will give you ten,' and he replied, 'Make it fifteen.' William retorted, 'I will do twelve, that is my limit!' and then the sergeant stated, 'It comes with two shire horses and a big unfriendly dog. They are all in the back stable. Would you like to see them?' 'Yes please, lead the way,' William remarked and in he went.

The big dog headed straight for him and he held out his hand and let him sniff all over him and he said to the dog face to face, 'Okay mutt, you are coming with me!' He patted his head quite roughly and the dog almost nodded his approval. Then he checked over the horses and gave them a good stroke and thought "these two beasts would probably pull a ton" and then he again spoke to the sergeant and said, 'Okay I will give you fifteen on one condition and that is could you keep them here for about another week!' The sergeant replied, 'Yes no problem,' and he explained why they were up for sale explaining to him that 'they belonged to an old gold miner, retired of course, who used to collect drunks and rowdies from the town for us but he passed away last week and we have no further use for them. That dog kept them well under control, so watch him he is a real nasty piece of work, but he took to you rather well,' and added, 'So you know about dogs?' William replied, 'Well not really. Only street dogs back in London,' and the sergeant then said, 'Thanks for the sale, see you tomorrow night during the renovation works and good luck on your journey to ... wherever!' Only then did he hand over the money.

He then thought while walking back to the shop, "I need an artist to write a display on the wagon to invite the people to see exactly what we do, and I know that very person. Young Nicole is a bit of an artist because I have seen her work when I visited her room just after she was employed by Fred and I reckon she would do this for me for free. I will speak to her in the morning." She said, 'Yes,' straight away and asked him, 'Why go into the west, isn't it a touch dangerous?' and he replied, 'The dark unknown doesn't fear me. I am only a simple man who just wants to improve himself in this vast country and I know no fear, so will you do it?' 'With pleasure,' she replied, 'but you will have to supply the paint and brushes,' and he stated, 'No problem,' and they both went to the stables that very evening to do their project. Mutt gave her a good sniff when she entered and William said to her, 'Take no notice to that old dog he always does that.' But that old dog knew the difference of a friend and a foe and he gently licked her leg and so he accepted her and left her well alone, and why?, because she brought him some sausages every evening when she came in, and on the sixth night she finished her last brush stroke. Then William told her, 'You have done an amazing job. Much better than I imagined. I will now take you to dinner out in the town but don't bother to change, it is not a posh place just somewhere to fill you up.' She gratefully accepted this offer and said, 'You are such a sweet man, how do you do it?' and he replied, 'I really don't know it is just who I am,' and off they went, still covered in paint and sawdust into some local joint for a few beers and a bite to eat and it was late in the night when they got back home to their places.

Of course he had walked her home to her room and she asked him in for a coffee but he refused and held up both hands and said, 'Sorry no can do I have a lot of things to prepare for tomorrow before I leave.' He then added, 'Meet me in the cafe at seven in the morning. I do need a little help to put some things in the wagon before I leave,' and she replied, 'Will do, but I look a bit of a mess at that time,' and he remarked, 'Just need your hands and legs, no worries, just turn up!' Off he went to check the horses in the stable and Mutt the dog was pleased to see him and bounded towards him and he told him a big trek was coming soon so "go back to sleep, there is a good boy". In the morning he met Nicole in the cafe as arranged and she asked, 'So just how old are you?' and he answered, 'Eighteen today but don't let on to the others I don't like any fuss!' Then she asked, 'So what drives you on?' and he replied, 'The fear of failure!' She smiled and remarked, 'No chance of that happening to you!' and then they packed the wagon full of his tools and equipment and a few other bits for the trip and now he was ready for Monday morning and he thought, "have I forgotten anything?" and did a final check.

Chapter Three

The next morning he got up just before the break of dawn and headed straight for that little cafe to have a hearty breakfast and now he was ready to roll. When he went into the stable the dog rushed at him to greet him but he was well prepared for that because he had brought him a big meaty bone and said to himself "now that will keep him well out of the way when I attempt to hitch up the horses", and it really did because Mutt took it into a little corner and just crunched away at it. Now he was ready to go and when he drove by the shop all the staff were out in front holding a big banner which read 'Bon Voyage' and that gave him even more determination to succeed in his trip to the west. As he headed through town he said to himself, "well here we go, it is do or die, just head for Ohio and beyond and there you will make progress".

It was a nice sunny morning and lots of people were out and about and many of them stopped him to asked "what is it all about" due to his odd colourful wagon and he pulled to a halt many times to explain and handed out some of the leaflets he had printed up. His stock answer was "I am out to correct people's eyesight with my new eyeglasses all the way from London England and we have on board ready-made reading glasses. Or we could provide you with a pair to suit your vision exactly but that will take about a week and you will have to pay in advance for them. Our shop is right in the middle of the town". Now that information got him quite a few orders itself and he had barely left the town and he was so full of new confidence and anticipation and a big smile. He continued on his extra-long journey to the west via Ohio. After he had tied up the wagon he looked for the wire office and after a few enquiries with some curious onlookers, he finally found it and sent a wire to its nearest office to the shop which read, 'Send two cases of plain reading glasses and a full pack of eye papers to this office here in Ohio on the first train out, William. Urgent!' Then he parked the wagon right in the middle of the town so that everyone could see it and that worked out well and only then he went for a bite to eat because it was a long time from his last meal. Just before he had left New York he made an arrangement with the office there to send any wire straight to the shop and that very evening in rolled the train with his goods and they dropped them off and he was there waiting to pick them up and then he went back to his wagon for a good night's sleep.

Now it was off to Indiana and Fort Wayne to fill some of the catalogue orders from his advert and there were quite a few, mainly from old people who were his bread and butter. So on he went to his next venue and it was quite a way. He checked the horses' shoes that they were fit for the journey and after they were fully watered and fed, he set off on his next trek and Mutt was quite happy just to trot alongside the wagon. Now and again he stopped for a quick wee –

and that was catching because both of the horses and the dog all went together and they were glad for that little break from the trek. Mutt was quite content with his new master after some tasty biscuits and a pat on his head so they rolled into Fort Wayne and were totally surrounded with a whole bunch of kids and some other interested adults who asked him a million questions. He spent quite a time with them and then he headed straight to the eating house for a coffee and a large slice of that cake he saw sitting on the counter when he had finished. Now he was ready for business and up they came one after another dying to hear some news from the outside world. But he was just concerned about their eyes, no idle chat, no news, just some new clients and he took them into his little sturdy wagon which was fully equipped with all his instruments along with a special chair to sit on while he took their readings.

When he joined the firm, just a mere lad of fourteen, quite underfed and feisty living on the streets of London, he was about average height and weighing about one hundred and thirty pounds. Now, at the grand old age of eighteen he was a strapping young lad standing about six feet tall and weighing in at two hundred and ten pounds all due to his life living in the attic above the shop, where he had decided to improve himself with some hard physical work, teach himself some guitar and think hard about his future.

And so now he travelled on to a place called Kansas. It was a long run to get there, but he made it just before dark and found the town was still quite lively. He had five immediate enquiries just from his advert in that magazine, then he booked into the local hotel and made himself noticeable by asking the barman if he knew anyone who needs specs in this town and that was quite a subject of interest. Four of his future clients were already in the bar at that time and he did them all in record time and asked one old couple, 'do you know a Mr and Mrs Jones?'. They told him they lived just around the back of the bank so off he went to check them over and they were really surprised to see him so quickly. Both got the eye test and paid him upfront for his service.

Next he was headed to Oklahoma to someone called Miss Little and it was an even longer trip to there. He travelled through the night and day to get there and both horses pulled through that long trek without stopping but then they pulled up outside the trading post and he dutifully saw them to service first after such a long trek and Mutt the dog was quite happy for a little rest as well. Now, before he had left the big city he decided he would need some firearms for this venture into the wild west. So he had popped into his favourite pawn shop to look for some suitable hardware for the journey and he picked out an old Henry rifle and a pair of pearl grip pistols complete with belt and one fine big hat to keep out that blazing sunshine on the trail. Then he spotted a big black Mac coat to keep out the dust from the trail. He went over to the counter and asked the man, 'So how much?' and he told him a price that sounded extortionate and William remarked, 'Not in a month of Sundays, give me a real good price or I will walk out with nothing. It is a Monday morning, you have got nil in your till, make both of us happy.' Then he headed to the door empty handed and the man called him back and said, 'Make it sixty dollars for all four items,' and he replied snappily, 'Done!' and added, 'See, now you feel better and me too thanks for that.' Now he was fully equipped for his journey and that big coat was an excellent choice because every time he hit a town he gave it a good shake and he was clean as a whistle and it covered his pistols.

When he had appeared in the trading post, the big lady running the store asked him, 'So where did you spring from?' and he then removed his hat and told her, 'I am here to see a Miss Little, she is interested to test some of my glasses, is she about?' and she answered, 'No not yet she is still in school but that is nearly over so she will be in any minute.' She then asked him, 'How did you get here? The train isn't due for another two hours,' and then added, 'You are not that old optician from Scarlet's are you?' and he gracefully replied, 'No I am that young optician, my name is William and I got here by wagon of course, come outside and see for yourself!' Out she went and exclaimed, 'Gosh you wouldn't miss that out here!' and he remarked, 'That is the idea, of course.' Then up breezed Miss Little and asked him directly, 'And you are? Is this your wagon? I think it is lovely and bright!' and then she told him, 'My name is, no kidding, Little Stick, and you are?' 'William!' he replied 'So you are not an old lady?' and she quickly retorted, 'No! And you are not an old man with whiskers are you?' Now after the introductions came the questions, one from each person quite quickly and Little Stick took the advantage first by asking him, 'Are you qualified for doing this process about eye testing?' and he replied, 'I am a fully qualified optometrist and I have the papers to prove it!' She then revealed that the glasses were not for her but for her mother and sister, who both did a lot of sewing in the camp for other people and then she revealed, 'My eyes really hurt after I gaze at the sun,' and he told her frankly, 'So don't look at it directly,' and she then said, 'Will you test them anyway?' 'Of course I will,' he replied and he sat her in his little chair and gazed into her eyes and remarked, 'God you have the most beautiful eyes I have ever seen in this world!' Then he slightly gave her an apology and said, 'Sorry I should never had said that!' and then she stood up and stated, 'Is that a compliment!' and he reluctantly answered, 'Yes I suppose it is,' and she boldly replied, 'Thanks, mister, it is a pleasure to meet you.' Off they went into her Indian camp on his wagon although this was not something he was prepared for and she gave him no clue as to who he might meet and he took a deep breath while rolling into the camp.

He first met her big sister and she asked him, 'Is there any ouch?' and he then looked at Little Stick and she gave him a pinch on the skin of his hand and said, 'She means pain,' and now he understood fully and told her, 'No not really, just look into the glass and tell me is it better or not.' Then he tried a few more and she said, 'That is it I can even read down to the last line,' and he took the readings and told her, 'Your eyes are not too bad just a little strained. I will give you a pair of ready-made glasses for now but you will need a proper pair made in our shop – it will take about six days to get here by train.' Next in came her mother and she did not trust any white man at all but she did take a seat in that strange chair and looked at her youngest daughter for some advice. She told her, 'No problem he is a qualified eye doctor. I have seen his papers from London, England. Just open your eyes widely when he asks you and then he will get a result to fix them with no pain.' The elderly lady did just that and said to William, 'Why are you so young doing this doctor thing?' and he told her, 'I am no doctor. Just tell me how you see through these glasses and I will correct your eyesight,' and added, 'I am an optometrist.' That meant nothing to this native woman, but she trusted her daughter's approval of him because she was the clever one in the family. Then Little Stick mentioned to him, 'There are quite a lot of people in the camp who just might need your skill and I will fetch them here one at a time.' But of course that didn't happen because any stranger in their camp drew a great attention from these people who lived in the middle of nowhere and eventually there was a bloody great line outside his wagon. He dealt with all of them with a smile and a check and even made a few other positive sales, though by then it was well into the night. He turned into his little cosy wagon for a good night's sleep and he rose early the next morning as usual. Then came a rap on his door and there stood Little Stick bright as a button, her hair neatly plaited as always bringing him a hot coffee and some fresh baked pancakes to meet the day with that big smile. Of course he invited her in and said to her, 'I would like to meet other Indians in camps nearby,' and added, 'Is it safe to go there without an invite?' and she then volunteered to go with him and said, 'They know me rather well. Some of them don't speak English but I know their language pretty well and I would like to be with you to see that you don't come to any harm.' He simply agreed to that and answered, 'Okay that would suit me thanks.' Then he remarked, 'You speak English very well!' and she replied shyly, 'Really!' and then told him, 'When I was a little girl I used to help Senga, you know the lady in the trading post, and one day some new settlers came into the store and asked her for a bag of flour and five eggs and an old rusty hand plough lying out at the front of the store. But then they told her 'we only have three dollars and this big book', and at the time I think it was called a dictionary and it was full of words in your language and Senga saw how my eyes lit up at that time and told them 'okay it is a done deal' and then she handed me that book. I read it cover to cover every day with the help of Senga and my teacher in my school, who also spoke English, and I picked out the most helpful words to speak to your people when that occasion arose. When I had finished my schooling my teacher asked me if I wanted to be her assistant and I said yes of course and that is why I speak this way.' When she had finished her tale he then gave her a little clap and said, 'Well done you must have been some clever little kid,' and she remarked, 'Is that another compliment from you?' and he replied, 'You bet it is!' and added, 'You really have the talent to fit into this new world and beyond.' 'What is this beyond?' she enquired, and he then revealed to her, 'The world is a really big place with many new things happening every day with you and your people benefiting from it!' Then she told him, 'I really like you!' and this remark he just let go and replied casually, 'I like you too,' and that was that.

Now it was off into the wild big open prairie lands and with not a trace of fear he slapped the reins onto his horses and placed his trusty rifle by his side and straight away ran into a small bunch of Indians just outside of the camp. Little Stick told him, 'No need for the rifle they are just curious, they want to check you out and have a little look to see what you are carrying,' and then she stood up and gave them a little wave. When they saw her, one of them waved back and said to his warriors, 'It is all right it is only Little Stick and a white man, let us go to check him out,' and they did that slowly because they knew that some white people were rather trigger happy. When they arrived, she said to him, 'No problem they are Chickasaw but don't make any sudden movement towards your gun!' and he replied, 'Don't worry I trust you fully, my sweet little apprentice.' They did have a good look around and asked her, 'So what is he selling?' and she replied, 'Good eyesight from the big city,' and they were pretty happy with that statement and one of them said, 'My old lady does need some new eyes, would he fix them?' She then turned to William and said, 'Now you have a new client we will go there it is not far,' and off they went into their camp and he did quite a few eye tests. She looked on in

24

amazement to see they accepted a white man to actually treat them for their eyesight and now she really liked him a lot and off they went even further into the plains. After a while he stopped the wagon and jumped out for a quick wee and she also needed one. He normally goes at the side of the wagon but now when a young lady was present he decided to go a little further away so that he was out of sight from her and he jumped into a slight dip in the sands. In there was also a mountain lion doing the same thing but when he saw this meal appearing, and it was alone, he jumped at him. But William just shouted, 'Mutt!' loudly and in he came like a fast steam train and he went straight to the lion's throat and he pulled him down and it was all over. Little Stick called, 'Is everything okay over there?' and he came back into view and remarked, 'It is now!' She then stated, 'You haven't done up your buttons yet!' and he said, 'There's a very good reason for that!'

Then they met a patrol of Buffalo Soldiers from a local fort and they all seemed to be quite pleasant and a few of them were quite interested with his reading glasses and offered to buy on the spot with real silver dollars. These men only earned fifty cents a day but to him a sale is just a sale so he took their money and then it was time to turn back to the Cherokee camp because she said to him, 'You must meet the elders in the camp because it is our custom.' When he approached them all with their big flowing headdresses and their stern faces and that witchdoctor hopping all over the place he took a deep gulp of his breath and stated, 'How, Big Chiefs,' and held up his right hand and said, 'Pleased to see you I come in peace, me not too familiar about your customs.' That brought quite a giggle from those present and some of those elders thought he was a madman reading too many cheap books of the Indian nation, but then Little Stick spoke to them and told them, 'He is a true man he knows nothing about our way of life. He is from England, a far-away country, and he is here to help us, not to steal our lands like many!' and that little speech did the trick and her dad was quite proud of her and he advised the other elders that he was a good straight white man and he was in favour of him.

The following day he took a further trip into the Great Plains to meet some other tribes and Little Stick went with him. He was quite happy with her company but not so much of the constant questions she asked about the big city and beyond to England. Good old Mutt took quite a shine to her because every time she came to see his new master she brought a little bag of meaty bones just for him and that meant to him one other person to protect in this big world. Now they rolled into the Creek camp and she called out loudly, 'Anyone here needs their eyes testing?' in their own language and of course that brought out quite a few old people who were more than curious about this brightly coloured wagon. She went on to explain to them, 'This man is an eye doctor from the big city and he will make you see better!' and then she handed out some of the reading glasses, with his permission of course, to some of the people and he then remarked to her in amazement, 'Now you would make a good salesman, or should I say saleslady.' Now this casual comment stuck in her head and there and then she planned to ask her dad "Can I go with him to the big city when he leaves here?" and she did just that in the evening when they got back.

Now her old man was no fool and he pondered slowly and quietly over this odd request while stroking his chin and the bridge of his nose and then asked her, 'What does he say to this?' and then she revealed, 'He knows nothing about it yet. I have yet to ask him.' Then he asked her, 'Do you really trust this young white man with your life?' and she replied, 'Totally, he is a good honest man not one bad thought in his head!' and he then told her, 'Okay, send him to meet me and your mother in our tepee the day before he leaves. I would like to have a little chat with him about your welfare,' and she answered quickly, 'Okay I will.'

Now William slept comfortably in his little wagon on a mattress which he had taken from the shop and he laid it on the floor at night along with his bedclothes which he rolled up during the day because there wasn't much room in there for all of his instruments. Good old Mutt kept his feet warm because he loved to be with him and lay at the bottom of the makeshift bed and the next day they were off to visit another camp. It was the Seminole camp not too far away and she told him, 'There is a man in here who makes the best bows in the whole country and he is a good friend of my old man and they are quite a friendly tribe so again, no need for guns,' and in they rolled and they were greeted like long lost friends because not many people ventured this far into the Great Plains. Once again she called out, 'Famous eye doctor from the big city is here to fix your eyes not too much dollars and he will even take yellow metal in exchange for his skill and even some furs. He served the Cherokee Nation well and quite a few others so if anyone is in need of new eyesight come and see us, we have got all the equipment necessary for the purpose!' William was even further impressed by this young girl's flair for selling and asked her, 'How would you like a job in the city selling eyeglasses for our firm in New York?' and she timidly replied, 'Is it quite far?' and he remarked, 'Very far but quite well paid, when you finish your training to be an optometrist.' Now she saw her chance and told him, 'You must speak to my dad first because he is the boss in our family,' and he did that the very next day. It wasn't easy because her dad had some set rules about his behaviour and he made him promise never to abuse her because of her young age although he never bothered to asked her about her age because he reckoned someone that clever must be older than she was. Travelling together into the Great Plains towards New York he was reluctant to ask such a question and he really enjoyed her presence on the long journey back home and she made no complaint on the way there. Before she got permission to go with him she packed some of her things and wrapped them up in a blanket; it contained two pairs of moccasins, a tomahawk, two spare dresses and her bow with a quiver full of arrows and a grey wolf skin jacket, which she dug out and wore for the journey along with a turquoise necklace which she thought made her look more attractive and he gracefully said so when she climbed aboard. Now he thought, "Good God, how will Fred react when I turn up with her at the shop and where will I put her". But that was not a problem right now.

Chapter Four

꧂

His two rear wheels were grinding quite noisily and he had to attend to them first. He pulled his horses to a stop, climbed out and got out the can of grease, applied it to all four of the wheels and waited for a few minutes until it sank in. Then he climbed back on and said to her 'That will do until we hit the next town' which was about fifty miles up the track and she thought "what a clever young man I am in real safe hands with him". There were small towns dotted all around the Great Plains but some of them were not safe places to stop in and she advised him on the way and told him "not there", and "not this one", "a few more miles to go then there is a quite large one, can these horses last out?" and he replied, 'Old Daisy and Maisy can go for miles at a fair pace.' Hearing this she remarked, 'But both horses are male why did you give them girls' names?' and he casually replied, 'They don't know they are girls' names, but they do respond to them if I call them over.' Then in they rolled to this town for a break in their journey and a bite to eat. But first they must attend to the horses and good old Mutt, so they headed to the nearest stable to sort them out and then see to themselves.

They slept in the wagon after that because he told her, 'No need to spend money when you have your own little private space, isn't that right, it is not too cold for you is it?' She then suggested, 'Not if we cosy up real close together!' Now there is his problem on this trip because of that vow he made to her dad and then he asked her enquiringly, 'So just how old are you?' and she dropped her head slightly and said, 'I am nearly fourteen!' He then exclaimed after that revelation, 'Holy moly I thought you were at least four years older!' and she quickly retorted, 'What is that, holy moly?' and he replied, 'It is like a shock to the brain!' and she remarked, 'Why is that?' He said, 'It is like you're out on the plains and you come across a baby bear out in the open and then his mother appears right in front of you!' and she quietly remarked, 'Oh that sort of thing.' She quickly changed the subject and said, 'Your dog is really a full bred wolf, did you know that? Look at his jaws and his eyes and those teeth they do not belong to some ordinary dog!' and he replied, 'Well I really didn't notice,' and then she revealed, 'I have met many wolves on the plains and believe me he is the real thing!' After that she added, 'You must have taken great care of him because he really trusts you.' Then he stated flatly, 'I must return you to your camp because I don't want a little kid with me on the trail,' and she screamed back at him, 'I am not a child I can look after myself pretty well.' 'You didn't think I was a kid when I helped you out with your sales on the trail and don't forget it is only a number so let us just carry on towards the big city!'

Now he had noticed that she had got a slight little frame but he presumed it was down to all that darting about she does and gave it no further thought. So all that idle chat from her did not distract him from the fact that she was only thirteen years old. Then her smart little brain ran out of pleasant things to say to him and she changed her tone and raised her voice to an ever higher level and called him straight to his face, 'You are just a stupid young white man with no vision at all on the future. Call yourself an optimist, not from where I am standing!' Just then he realised he was a touch petty about her age and gave her a little smile but he didn't say sorry and then she told him quietly, 'I need a little cuddle just before I settle down to sleep because all that fuss over nothing makes me a bit edgy.' He obliged with much caution because he had never had a girl that close to him in the past. He then removed the rolled up mattress from the corner and laid it on the floor along with a few blankets and she dived straight on it, still fully dressed of course because this was just as new to her as it was to him. He slowly removed his jacket gun belt and boots and then snuffed out the oil lamp hanging on the wall and slipped in beside her, straight away. She then cosied up real close to him and now he had nowhere to go because it was a very small mattress. She thought it was a pleasant bit of cosy fun but for him it was quite an awkward moment because he had never been in this situation before although he did find that it was rather pleasant until she wrapped her legs around his. Now he had a big problem and he then pretended to sleep but she wouldn't let that stop her and she began prodding him awake and then he told her frankly, 'Now that is enough, we have got a long day ahead of us, get some shuteye, there is a good girl, otherwise I will take you straight back to your camp now!' and that sharp short message did the trick and she quietly rolled over and went to sleep and now she knew who was the boss on that trail.

The next morning she was up at the crack of dawn, wrapped herself up in a blanket, went outside, lit a fire, put the pot on and made some coffee and hot pancakes for breakfast. He rose about ten minutes later due to the aroma and she brought them into the wagon to a delighted young hungry man and now she knew that they were not heading back to her camp, because he had now lost that stern look on his face. They got dressed, went down to pick up the horses and Mutt was loping towards her at a great pace and she gave him a big grin and patted his head.

Then he told her, 'It is a long trek to the next big town we will have to sleep in the wagon for two nights before we get there,' and she chirpily replied, 'I don't mind as long as you keep me warm during the night.' He also said to her, 'Now and again I would like you to take the reins of the horses if you don't mind,' and she remarked, 'I will do that, it is my pleasure,' and then he told her, 'But do look out for rocks on the trail.' Again she replied, 'Will do.' By then the dust had really built up and he gave her a special pair of blue tinted glasses which he kept in that little leather bag of his and she put them on and said, 'This is truly wonderful I can see through the dust and the sun in my eyes doesn't really bother me!' By now she had a real crush on him, much stronger than before and that night they rolled the wagon to a stop in the middle of nowhere and their only food supply was some bread and cheese and an apple and she thought "tomorrow we will dine like kings and queens" and decided to hunt some game. She did just that and felled a young deer with her bow and took it to him proudly and he then asked her, 'So how do we cook it?' and then she stated, 'I am a Cherokee maiden, watch me!' With that she took out her skinning knife from her belt and sliced off the skin with speed, then she laid down all the different parts and asked him, 'Which part do you like best in a nice stew?' and then she salted the rest for later. Now he was really impressed and no longer thought that she was a burden on the trek home.

That night they ate well, washed down with a few beers, which he always restocked in every town he visited, and went to sleep despite the howling wolves through the night. Mutt slept just at the back door as usual crunching away happily on that bone she gave him after their meal. The skin of the animal she scraped clean and salted as well and pinned it on the outside of the wagon. The next morning they both rose at the break of dawn and watered their horses, had a quick coffee and off they went towards the next big town. It was a nine-hour stint and no big problems yet, but then they ran into a small bunch of not-so-pleasant trail hands who were driving a cattle herd in the opposite direction to them. They wanted to have a little fun and their herd was out in front of them so they tried to stop the wagon but William took no chances and pulled out his Henry and told them to clear off and Little Stick slipped back into the wagon for her bow and quiver. She opened the back door and let go two arrows and both of them hit their target and she told Mutt to "stay there don't move" and he did and William up front slapped the reins and egged his horses on to a faster pace but they couldn't outrun the two lone riders. Then William fired a shot but he missed and she quickly went up front, let go one more arrow and hit one rider right in the belly and the other one pulled back to help his companion and they were now free to continue their journey without a mark. In they rolled to town and he said to her, 'Must find a blacksmith. Daisy is limping a little on the left side. Might need some new shoes. In fact I will take both of them because it is still a long way to go,' and so then he unhitched the horses and asked a local, 'Where is the blacksmith?' He replied, 'About five minutes away just straight down this road, you couldn't miss it, big horseshoe sign above it.' 'Thanks,' said William and went down with the horses towards it while Little Stick just sat on the step on the doorway and swung her legs and glanced around a town she hadn't been to and Mutt was happily sniffing around the back of the wagon to discover new smells. Up came a couple of young cowboys straight towards the wagon and she smelled trouble before they even reached her as they were laughing and swearing and making strange little noises. She withdrew the skinning knife, which she always kept in her belt and said to them, 'That is close enough just leave me be!' and one of them said to the other, 'Listen, a little squaw who speaks English, what is the world coming to? Me I like a little fun with her, how about you?' Then she said, 'Mutt!' loudly in a tone that he was well aware of and in he bounded with teeth baring and jaws snapping and he went straight to his gun hand and bit it clean through, and the other one said, 'I will shoot it clean through his head!' Up came William leading the horses, but when he saw the situation he let them go and both of them ran over the two men in their haste to get back to their young lady who feeds them well. Only then did William and Little Stick restock their provisions and have a quick bite to eat in a local cafe.

Now this next leg of their trek would take about five days provided they didn't stop in any of the small towns on their way, because he had a reason to get back to New York pronto and he bought enough provisions to last that length of time, which sufficed along with the venison they had on board already. Little Stick also purchased some more salt and some soap to wash with although he wasn't that keen on her purchases because he thought she smelled all right as she was but she insisted and he let it go.

The more she travelled with him the fresher she got and he resisted her on every cold night but there was no place to go other than the cold floor and that was not a good idea out on the Great Plains because it was far too cold. So he cuddled her as much as she wanted and he turned his back when she asked for more and went to sleep and this went on throughout this long trek, but he had some sweet dreams about her although he didn't know why, but that didn't bother him. Next they arrived in a place called Ohio and he decided to take the train for the rest of the journey so he dropped into the rail station and asked, 'Is there a train to carry a wagon and two horses to New York?'

and the young clerk answered, 'Yes there is, it is due to leave here at nine in the morning.' William answered, 'Fine I will book it with two people on board thank you,' and now it was time to eat, so off they went to find a nice little place to fill their hungry bodies and they came across a sweet little cosy restaurant.

There was a rather stern looking lady at the door and she addressed William saying, 'You cannot bring your Indian slave in here,' and he retorted with a smile and said to her, 'Tell her that, she understands English pretty well!' Then Little Stick followed him in and that lady blocked her entrance and off she went like a stick of dynamite and told her quietly, 'You are in my way you ignorant and downright ugly invader I have more right than you to be in this country!' Now that was the fizzing bit and the big bang came straight after it and this stuck up lady remarked with some shock, 'Well I have never heard such a language.' Then Little Stick really screamed at her saying, 'Look lady you are the bloody foreigner not me and I am no slave to no one!' Out came the owner from behind the till to find out what was the ruckus about and he asked the lady to stand aside and then waved in the girl and said to William, 'Don't worry, she is new to the job,' and led both of them to a table in a corner before remarking to Little Stick, 'You have a fire like an Italian just like me and that I like, so what will you have? The wine is on the house if you have a meal.' She grinned at him and remarked, 'Two of the best meals you have got; we just came in from Oklahoma and I am starving hungry along with my new boss,' and William said nothing throughout except, 'Thank you,' and then he opened the wine and said, 'Cheers.' Up came two massive steaks with all the trimmings and after they had finished she remarked, 'I feel much better after that.' Then the owner arrived with the bill and William gave him a dollar tip and he said, 'Thank you, kind sir!' and added, 'So where are you heading? 'New York to my shop,' William replied, and they left and went to the wire office to let the shop know they would be there soon and while he arranged loading the horses and wagon onto the train she went to pick up their tickets.

The young clerk at the station had never seen a real Indian girl in his life and began chatting her up and she told him, 'Don't waste your time on me I have already got a big white man,' and then she leaned over the counter and planted a kiss on his cheek and he remarked, 'I never knew Indian girls were so pretty!' and added, 'I would never wash that side ever again,' and gave her a big grin. Out she went with that satisfied smile and asked William, 'All ready to go?' and he replied quickly, 'All done, we will take Mutt in with us!' and on they went into the carriage. It was quite a long journey but of course a lot quicker than the wagon and no rocks to look out for on the way. They were sitting comfortably on the way there in their separate blankets wrapped around them and then along came a stroppy woman and said to him, 'You cannot allow that squaw on this train, tell her to leave!' William replied, 'Tell her that to her face!' and Little Stick sprung up and faced this rather posh woman and told her, 'I have got a ticket for this train and I intend to finish my journey in peace, so you can just leave, you piece of work and you should wear a bag over your head to hide your unpleasant tongue!' This lady was quite taken aback with this verbal attack and walked off back to her seat and William then remarked to her, 'I truly admire the way you spit fire!' and she answered, 'You know that rhymes, it sounds like something lethal, so is that how you see me? 'Absolutely without question!' he replied and she then remarked, 'Good I don't take no rubbish from no one if they're nasty to me!' To this he responded, 'So let us catch some sleep for the rest of this journey with a nice cuddle,' and then they rolled into New York.

Chapter Five

~~~

Slowly and surely he grew more fond of this young girl's attitude and manner but he didn't dare show it because of that vow he made to her old man. He had never felt like this before but he had yet to learn and he liked this feeling quite a lot. Now it was time to unload the wagon from the train and hitch up the horses and head for the stable and then unpack their things and return to the shop. But at least they had made it back safely in one piece and he thought how lucky there was a whole team in the station to help him to do just that. After that they unloaded their things from the wagon into the shop and took it back to the stable where they gave the horses a good rub down before they left. Then it was time to ask her about her opinion of the big city and he did just that. While walking back to the shop, he asked her, 'So what do you think about the big city?' and she replied, 'Well the station was quite a sight but the streets out here are a touch mucky and smelly but yes I like it. So how far is your shop?' and he said, 'Not too far away.' Then she asked him, 'Your big boss, does he like a little joke?' and he replied, 'Sometimes what did you have in mind?' and she nonchalantly replied, 'Oh nothing too important.'

Then in they walked into the shop together because she did not enter the shop when they unloaded the wagon on purpose as she wanted to make an entrance. All the staff were there waiting to greet William and Little Stick walked up to Fred and stated with a serious face, 'How, big white boss!' and held up her hand and he was completely speechless. Then she stated, 'I am here to work for you to become an optimist!' and Fred then gazed at William and asked him, 'Is she for real?' and he remarked, 'She is one really clever girl and that is exactly what I did in the Indian camp in front of all of the elders. And she does speak perfect English!' Little Stick then remarked, 'I thought that was rather funny didn't you?' and now he got the gist of her and gave a short little laugh and shook her outstretched hand and now she was smiling and all the rest of the staff thought that was quite amazing to turn Fred that quickly into a happy mood. So now she was accepted and that was no trick, all part of her approach to people she didn't know which was exactly why William brought her there because he had the knowledge to recognise the right sort of people who had that driving force within.

Aah, but wait a second, it was not his idea to bring her along it was hers, because she made herself quite useful on the trail for that exact purpose just to see the big wide open world of the white man in New York and beyond. It had been an easy thing for her to persuade her parents to let her go with no conditions. Now her dad knew that his clever little eagle was ready to fly from the nest into the great beyond and with a nod of his wife he let her go with this white man because he trusted him and his honest approach. But he did get William's word on oath that he would never abuse her while she was in his care and that is something to live up to with a fourteen year old girl ready to explore a new way of life and he did just that with gritted teeth and with sheer will power.

Then he thought now where do I put her, and Nicole almost read his thoughts and said, 'She could stay with me in my tiny room and my bed is big enough for two.' He gasped a sigh of relief and said to her, 'Thank you I am sure she will behave properly,' and then Little Stick remarked, 'I always behave that way do not make assumptions on my part,' and everybody in the room realised this was no stupid young girl. She grinned at Nicole and said, 'Thank you for your offer it would be a pleasure to stay with you and I do rise early so you wouldn't have to wait to get into the bathroom.'

Then William conferred with his two male colleagues about the catalogue trade and Fred told him, 'Well, frankly orders just flowed in day after day, big ones and little ones, and that little chap from the wire office didn't complain because they generated so much business for them. So I left you on full pay for that time you were away and I must congratulate you for your clever idea about going out to the west, you are a braver man than me.' Then he added, 'So how were the Indians out there?' and William replied, 'Really quite friendly and helpful but nowhere near as clever as the one I brought back!' Fred remarked to him, 'We need more staff due to the volume of work you have brought in and that young girl may just fit in nicely as she is quite smart I have noticed, so what is the score with her?' He replied, 'She just wants to improve herself. She is now living on a reservation in Oklahoma in the middle of nowhere and she got her parent's permission to come with me so it is all above board,' then he added, 'She is excellent with young children and that is surely a bonus for us and the shop!' Fred then asked him, 'So what is your gain out of this?' but he didn't respond to that probing question because he didn't know the answer. Then he took Little Stick out of the shop and into his favourite little cafe for a quick coffee to refresh themselves after that long journey and have a private little chat on their future in New York. She was truly overwhelmed with the sheer size of the city and the volume of the people living there but she had no intention to turn her back on such an opportunity and she just grinned at him and said, 'I simply love it here. I want to become an optimist just like you.' He corrected her and stated, 'The word is optometrist!' and she replied, 'Oh I cannot get my native tongue around that word I much prefer optimist, your word is far too tricky to say.'

The next morning he was up as usual bright and early to open the shop and let the girls in and all was nearly back to normal except there was that little Indian girl with nothing to do. But Nicole soon fixed that and she gave her a cloth and asked her to wipe down the desks and windows while she organised some files and paperwork on her desk and come lunchtime William called over Nicole and asked her to take Little Stick to the shops to get her some suitable clothes to wear in the shop and he also gave her a fifty dollar bill and said, 'That should cover it.'

She asked him, 'Could we also get some lunch out of this? and he replied, 'Yes sure, no problem!' So off they went shopping and Nicole told her, 'In the first shop you pick and I will approve – that is how it works and if I say "no no" you will put it back. It is really a little game okay,' and she replied, 'Okay will do.'

When they entered the posh shop one lady in the shop went, 'Oooh look what just came in!' to another young assistant and both of them turned their backs and carried on arranging the window. But Nicole was no fool so she waved the fifty dollar bill to the man standing behind the counter and that did the trick. Over he came and said, 'Well, ladies, how can I help you?' and then Nicole explained to him, 'This young girl has just started as an assistant in Scarlet's opticians, you know the big shop with the gold lettering on the window, and she needs two full smart outfits to suit her position, but nothing too glaring.' After a quick glance at her he remarked, 'She is a size six, of course, we can fit her out with pleasure. Come with me and I will show you some suitable attire to suit such a position.' Then Nicole warned him, 'She speaks perfect English by the way. Don't think she's some dumb girl. She will pick out what she likes not you,' and he got that message loud and clear and asked this young Indian girl politely, 'So just starting out a new career in the big city, where are you from?' and she replied with a smile, 'Oklahoma! So let us get started. I just love those big flowing dresses but I bet they are difficult to walk in!' That remark too made him quite wary and he decided to take a more delicate approach to this pretty young lady and she sensed his change in attitude in a split second and Nicole then stopped squirming while she stood there and watched the pair come to terms.

They finished up with some suitable attire for the purpose and all picked out by herself. Just before they left she noticed a fine Panama hat in the window and said, 'I will take that also thank you, kind sir!' and gave him a big smile. Now he was really delighted with that remark and then he saw them to the door and called over the two assistants and asked them, 'Why wouldn't you serve them? They were nice polite girls. Remember money is money, no matter what they look like. That was a big sale and bang goes your commission, so put your noses back in position.'

Then off they went to a nice lunch with his money to spend and Nicole had a fine way to do just that entering one very fine restaurant in town and asking the waitress, 'Give us two meals of the house along with a bottle of fine wine.' Then they dumped their bags at the side of their table, all because William had set no time on their shopping trip and she was determined to make this little venture a real pleasure for their new employee and young Little Stick felt completely at ease with Nicole throughout. While back in the shop the three men were sitting downstairs eating their lunch because they had no time to go out on his first day back and William told the other two, 'I think we should run the advert in the catalogue till the end of the year,' and both of them agreed on that because it was bringing in a lot of sales. Then in came the two girls from their shopping trip and Tim remarked lightly, 'So now we have a fashion show!' and Little Stick retorted, 'No not now, far too much to do I need a chance to get in the mood to show off my finery, wait until tomorrow. Give a girl a chance to prepare for such an occasion!' And so it was back to the normalities of the day. Then Nicole handed back to William the change of the bill he gave her and told him, 'She picked very well and you couldn't believe just how she looked in those dresses. She is quite a little honey. Put her on the front desk and people would line up just to see her sitting there; you have picked a good one there but of course you already knew that!' But he didn't reply to that and went on with his chat to Fred and Little Stick looked at him thoughtfully and asked herself, "just what is he planning for the future. He is a real deep one. Did I make the right choice coming all the way out here with him? Now that I will have to mull over a touch more". And then Nicole gave her something to do in the office.

At six am the next morning both girls jumped out of bed and headed to the washroom at great haste before anyone could get there and started to prepare for her big entrance day. They got washed, fixed their hair and did their business and headed straight back to their room to dress. Little Stick had had the good sense to have laid it out the night before and that well-fitting light blue one was her pick and Nicole truly thought she had made the right choice. Then she asked her, 'Can you button it up for me on the back?' and then she admitted, 'It feels rather strange to have this on.' Nicole then said to her, 'Now try the shoes,' and she did, but she dare not look in the mirror on the wall. Then she put on the mackintosh coat that William gave to her and said, 'Now that feels better,' and then on goes the Panama hat and she said to her newly found friend, 'Now I am ready for breakfast and to face the world!' So they then popped into their little cafe which they used all the time and Emilio the Spanish waiter who had quite an eye for pretty girls asked Nicole, 'So who is this little beauty with you?' and she replied with a grin, 'This is that little Indian girl.' He then went on to say, 'She is even more pretty today,' and Nicole retorted, 'Hands off, you Latin lover, you have got no chance with her!' He put up both hands in the air and replied, 'Okay no offence just such a pretty lady,' and then he took their order and Little Stick just sat there and smiled throughout his feeble attempt. After they had finished, she stood up, took off her coat and gave him a little twirl in her new outfit and everyone in the cafe gave her a little applause for that gesture and Nicole realised now she has regained her confidence in her new unfamiliar clothes and said to herself "what a girl". They headed to the shop and in she breezed with a bigger smile than usual, opened her coat for all to see and Fred was first to comment and told her, 'You look remarkable. I am amazed. You will fit in here easy without any problem,' and added, 'Now everyone back to work!' William was truly astonished by the transformation before him and told her, 'You see you can do it, just stay as sweet as you are!' and then he kissed her on the forehead which caught her by surprise and she answered with a smile, 'Well thank you, kind sir,' and thought to herself "he does like me after all so what is his problem? It isn't me. It must be something in his past, that is it, I am sure". Then it was all back to business before the orders came rolling in from the catalogue via the wire service. In came the boy from that service with some more new business and the three went upstairs and Nicole saw to him and Little Stick was now manning the reception desk nearest the door.

After about ten days sitting on the front desk, which involved directing people to Nicole and Roseanne and showing off their latest frames, she got a bit bored and went upstairs to see Fred for a little chat and told him frankly, 'I am not happy with my position, will you let me train to be an optimist from start to finish along with all the assembly work?' He said to her, 'Young lady you can start tomorrow morning but wear something simple not your best clothes and be sharp upstairs in the workshop at eight,' and she replied, 'I will, Mr Fred.' So that was settled, and the next morning she turned up in her Indian dress complete with plaits in her hair to keep it out of the way and Nicole queried her that same morning in their room, 'Just what are you doing, you are not leaving surely after such a short time?' 'Certainly not' she replied, 'I am now in training to be a fully fledged optimist!' and Nicole then remarked to her, 'Listen baby you don't need to try for that, you are already an optimist.' But Little Stick still could not say optometrist and of course Nicole didn't know that.

Up she went into the workshop and was ready for

any task Fred put forward. She was fully skilled with her hands and up came the assembly of the frames and she did it skilfully, well before the given time he set for her and then the polishing of the glass inserts which needed just a little buffing to get them just right. Tim then remarked, 'That is just remarkable in such a short time,' and Fred told the young lady, 'You will fit in here like a spider in her web!' and William already knew that from the beginning and said to her, 'You will go very far and I will always be with you,' and after that little trial she went downstairs and changed into her fancy clothes once again to greet their clients in. Nicole then asked her, 'So how did it go?' and she confidently replied, 'It was a piece of cake!' And so on to a new career in the big city for her because now she knew she was in favour of the big boss in the shop and after two years she had fully qualified as an optometrist.

Chapter Six

But there was one little problem and that was she couldn't actually say the word optometrist. Now she was just barely sixteen and eager to try her new skill out on some of their clients, but Fred was a real stickler on the process and he insisted that she must say the given title before he could hand over the diploma to her and she told him, 'I just cannot get my tongue around that word!' William said to her, 'Just give it a go,' and added, 'Where do you come from?' and she replied, 'You know that already!' and then he asked her, 'Which tribe do you belong to?' and she answered, 'Why Cherokee!' and then he stated, 'Now in the beginning they are all foreign words to you how did you learn them?' and then he added, 'By breaking them down right!' She then explained, 'But they are all known words to me, not like that one!' and he then told her, 'Now it is part of your vocabulary because you are in that profession just break it up into four separate pieces!' She gave him one of those looks, took a deep breath and out it came, 'Optometrist!' with no hesitation. Fred then handed her the document and wished her well and William then kissed her on the cheek and gave her a gentle hug and now she was fully in, and had the paper to prove it and up came that smile of glee. She then repeated it in her head over and over again, just in case she had forgotten it.

She was then promptly allocated by Fred to testing all the children and difficult old people who came into the shop and with her manner, she quickly sorted them out. Nicole asked her, 'Just how do you do it with no screaming tantrums or any fuss?' and she remarked, 'Just make it a little game. I used to help my teacher back in school make it a little game. Kids and old people just love a little game not a boring task and then they sit quietly and try out the lenses and say yes or no which one suits them it is really a pleasant task for me and for them,' and Nicole then said to her, 'You know I might just try it out your way,' and she replied, 'Please do, I am flattered you see it my way.' Then it came to Nicole's next client and she was a rather nervous lady who couldn't read at all without squinting and Nicole asked her to sit down and place her chin on the rest and said to her, 'So what is the problem? Let me check your vision. Now look directly into the light then move your eyes left then right,' and said to her, 'Okay I spot it.' Then over came Little Stick and she told the lady, 'Don't worry, there is no pain involved just breathe deeply and do what the lady says,' and Nicole then told her, 'You will need quite strong glasses and then you will see much better in the future.' Little Stick then revealed, 'I even taught my dad to speak English and that was something else. He just refused to utter a single word but I kept on with it and now he even likes a few English jokes and that is what I call progress.' Nicole then remarked lightly, 'You really are a pushy little bitch aren't you?' and this remark she brushed off lightly and said, 'If you don't try you will never succeed!'

At five o'clock that same day a mother came in with two children and she addressed the lady and asked politely, 'Okay which one of them?' and she replied, 'Both of them but they think it is a waste of time.' Little Stick responded, 'No big problem let us test both of them. There is no cost for testing so there is no extra outlay on your part,' and the little boy said, 'Let me go first.' 'Now that is not very polite,' she told him, 'little girls always go first in my book. Now let us play a little game. Do you both know the paper and scissors game? Let us do that and we will see who is first.' At this suggestion his little sister piped up gleefully, 'Yes let us do that,' and on they went and the little girl won with a rock against scissors and she was quite pleased and all the tension had gone between them. The mother enquired, 'How did you do that?' and she explained, 'I used to help my teacher back in school in Oklahoma to encouraged the young to listen in lessons,' and the lady then remarked openly, 'So you are an Indian, that is why you have such a good colour?' and Little Stick replied proudly with that smile, 'I am a full blooded Cherokee. One of my bosses brought me here to teach me to be a fully qualified optometrist and here on the wall is my diploma. I only got it two months ago!' Then she pointed it out to her and then told the lady the results of the tests and explained to her, 'That is why they are not good at school.' 'So when can I pick them up?' the lady asked and she replied, 'About four days. I will rush them through as they really need them so they can progress through school.' Nicole when passing said to her, 'Another satisfied client,' and she replied with a smile, 'Why of course that is why I am here!' and she took the results upstairs and gave them to William.

The next six months zipped by and her confidence in the shop increased more every time she handled a new client both young and old. But there was no progress on the romantic side with William and she had tried every trick in her attempts to try to make herself more attractive to him but he just wasn't biting on the hook. She generally took this problem to Nicole because she valued her opinion and she suggested, 'Maybe he bats for the other side. He treats you like a little sister, true think about it!' and then she added, 'No that is not possible, not him!' Little Stick asked, 'Explain please?' and Nicole said, 'No need, it is just an old cricket game back in England, no need to worry about it.' Then down came Fred and said to her, 'You, young lady, are due for a rise in pay after all that business you brought into the firm in the last six months!' and Little Stick then quickly enquired, 'Can I have a week off to go to see my dad back in Oklahoma?' This request didn't faze him one bit and he replied, 'Sure but you will need a little more cash to do that. I will supply that. So when are you going?' and she remarked, 'I need to go just before the fall, after that it is much too cold!' she remarked, and then he asked her, 'Does William know that?' and she then dropped her head and replied, 'Not yet!' Now she had a plan, but she had not yet thought it through because she had a tendency to grab the bull by its horns. The day before she left Fred asked her, 'Are you going alone?' and she replied, 'No not really, I will take Mutt along with me,' and that unexpected answer was not the one he was expecting and then he asked her, 'So William doesn't know you are going alone?' and she replied, 'No I will tell him later.' she replied, 'Anyway he is far too busy in the workshop.'

When she did finally tell him he nearly hit the roof and said to her, 'You are far too young to travel alone on the train by yourself!' and she retorted, 'Listen, mister, I am sixteen and a half and I can look after myself pretty well and I am taking Mutt along too!' Now he had to figure out the proper solution because he had given his word to her dad not to let her get in any danger and not to mislead her, for instance not to take advantage of her youthful way and so now he had to just let her go on her own. But he did accompany her to the train station and gave her fifty silvers dollars for her dad as a gift from him and in she went and had a little chat with the guard and she got her dog a free ride.

Chapter Seven

꧁

It was one long ride to Oklahoma on the train but not quite as long as by trail. She took with her a small valise and a large leather case which she bought from a local street market and when she got into the carriage she dumped the larger one on the floor beside her chosen place and sat down. Up came the conductor for a little chat because the train was still filling up with passengers and he asked her, 'So how far are you going?' and she replied, 'To Oklahoma to the Indian camp there.' Then he enquired, 'You are not some official, surely you are much too young for that?' and she scoffed back to him, 'No you silly boy!' and then revealed to him, 'I am going to visit my family there. I am a full blooded Cherokee but I now have a position in New York as a fully qualified optometrist so I test eyes for people who need glasses just like those ones you are wearing.' Then he enquired, 'So how did you land a job like that from your camp?' and she then smiled and said, 'Just pure luck I guess!' but he enquired further and asked her, 'So will you stay in the big city or go back home to work?' and she just shrugged and said, 'Well I really don't know. It is not up to me, it is up to William.' Then he got called away by some passengers who didn't know where to put their big bags and he told them, 'I will put them in the van. Have you got them labelled?' and they all replied, 'Yes we have.' Now all the passengers were on and he could relax until the next stop and so he sat next to this young lady. Mutt raised his head and gave a little growl and Little Stick advised him, 'Do not sit too close to me he is a touch protective!' so he moved to the adjacent seat and Mutt dropped his top lip to cover his baring teeth and she gave him a little pat on his head.

She was now wrapping herself into a big blanket she had brought and was ready to sleep and Mutt had the same thought and after a few more stops the old conductor was again checking people's tickets but he left the young lady sleeping because he had already done hers. Then after a fair way he saw she had unwrapped herself and gave her a call saying, 'Next stop after this one is yours,' and added, 'I will get your big bag, but this is not a station stop it is in the middle of nowhere but I have also got some goods to drop off so there will be a wagon waiting there to take you on.' And she replied, 'Fine by me thank you, kind sir.' That line always did the trick and she loved saying it because she always got a big smile back.

So next he brought out a little step for her to alight safely and there waiting beside the tracks was a wagon from the trading post. Who was driving it of course but one of the boys from her school although he didn't recognise her and he asked her, 'So are you a friend of Senga? She didn't tell me you were there.' Then she removed her Panama hat and shook down her pigtails and said to him, 'Look closely at me I am your teacher's assistant. It is me, Little Stick, but don't tell the people in the village I want to surprise them okay, not a word,' Once they arrived at the trading post Mutt ran straight in well before she had the time to step off and Senga said to the dog, 'Now you I know, so who is with you?' and in she breezed and said, 'It is only little old me!' Senga was truly taken aback and uttered, 'My God you look amazing, so you are obviously doing rather well in the big city!' Little Stick replied, 'Yep but I miss my family and I need a little chat with my dad,' and Senga enquired, 'Is there something wrong?' and she replied, 'Not quite sure. Things don't quite work out as planned.' Senga remarked, 'So tell me about it,' and added, 'Did you bring some of those ready-made glasses with you?' and she replied, 'Yep a whole case. Is that enough?' Senga remarked, 'Nice one, they will fly out the door; thank you for thinking ahead,' and Little Stick then asked her, 'Can I change into my old clothes here? I don't want my dad to see me like this.' Senga replied, 'Don't be silly, why not? You look super nice stay just as you are. He will be delighted to see you are getting on with your life. Have a coffee, sit down and tell me all about New York!' Senga then sent her boy with the wagon to pick up her family in the village and then asked her one more time about life in the big city. She obliged and showed her the diploma she had gained through the work she had done there and Senga was really impressed with that and said to her, 'Good girl I knew you had it in you,' and then in walked her dad. He wouldn't wait for the wagon and just jumped on his horse and went on ahead and he asked Senga quizzically, 'Well where is she?' and she retorted, 'She is around somewhere, you know what she is like she's always poking around the store.' Then he turned to the well-dressed lady and asked her, 'Have you seen a little Indian girl around?' and she remarked back to him, 'You mean Little, Stick!' Then she took off her hat and shook down her hair and replied, 'It is really me, look into my eyes. See your little girl!' and he took a sharp gasp with an odd look on his face and said, 'You really fooled me that time!'

Little Stick then asked Senga, 'Can we use your back room for a little chat?' and she replied, 'Yes sure go for it.' Now this room was small and private tucked right in the back of the store and she revealed to her dad, 'You and me need a little chat about William pronto. He just doesn't react to my approaches in any way and I think he is the wrong man for me. He barely touches at all!' To this her father answered, 'Ah, that is a good thing, he is a man of his word. You see we made a little pact before you left that he would never misuse you because of your age and he has kept his word to me, that is a good thing and that is why I let you go with him to the big city. He is a good man unlike some who I wouldn't care to mention,' and she then gave a big sigh of relief and a big hug to her dad and said to him, 'You know I wouldn't like to lose him, thank you, Dad, for clearing my head full of useless thoughts. You are a very wise man!' She gave him a little kiss on his cheek and so they went back into the main store and first in was her big sister Tasillaqua who exclaimed with delight when she saw her, 'Well well my sweet prodigal little sis, the one you couldn't miss. Well, you have obviously done well for yourself so how is the big city?' and gave her a great hug and said, 'You look real swell just love your clothes and I adore your hat!' Next in came her mum quickly followed by Mutt and she went straight up to her and grabbed her with both hands and uttered, 'Mamma mia what have they done to my little baby?' and then she looked her all over and asked her, 'Are you eating well?' but Little Stick didn't reply and just gave her a big hug. Then Senga reappeared from the stockroom and enquired, 'Well all done, everything in order, all happy, me must go back to work and drum up a little trade,' and added, 'My boy will take you back.' Little Stick asked her, 'I must change into my old dress. Before I go there, can I change in your little room?' and in there she took the silver dollars out of the valise for her dad. So off they went back into the village where they had prepared for her one big event to welcome her back. Now that she wasn't prepared for but she was well pleased to see all of her old friends and kinfolk.

They hadn't known when she was coming but when her sister heard from the boy driving the wagon that she was here, off she went to get all the children in the village to assemble where the wagon normally stops and when they saw her in the wagon they let out a mighty scream of welcome and that brought out in her a few tears of happiness. She then threw herself off the wagon and straight into the excited kids without any hesitation and it was lucky for her that she didn't weigh that much as they all managed to bear her little frame without dropping her. She shouted, 'I am back. It is me. Really. Go on touch me!' and many of them did. Then there were dancing and singing and a few little demonstrations with tomahawk throwing and bow and arrow shooting and she was mighty good at all of them. Eventually she settled down and had something to eat with a little lemonade to wash it down and stated to her people, 'Lovely to come back but I won't be staying too long.' After it had all died down Tasillaqua told her, 'You will be sleeping with me tonight on the floor is that all right?' and she remarked back, 'No problem with me. I ain't no white lady. If I can shut my eyes and have a little cuddle that is good enough for me.' Then big sister enquired, 'So is this white man a good cuddle?' and she replied, 'Not half, he has a nice tight body and he is lovely and warm on a cold night on the plains. It is a long way to New York and I couldn't pick a better companion to take me there and he is not boring at all and we chatted all the way but he is a touch shy and I found out why!' Tasillaqua said, 'Go on tell me tell me?' and she answered, 'He made a promise to our dad that he would never misuse me because of my age. Of course he never knew it and when I told him I was coming up to fourteen he nearly hit the roof and he almost took me back to our village. But then I made myself quite useful on the trail and that idea flew out of the window,' and her sister then remarked, 'You really are a clever little girl aren't you!' Then Little Stick told her, 'It is my first one and I am sticking to him like glue and do you know he has never made an improper move towards me in the past two years. Tell me, do you know any young buck would do that?' and she flatly replied, 'Absolutely not!' and then she added, 'So when are you going back?' and Little Stick replied, 'Maybe the day after tomorrow. I must catch that train in the afternoon.'

When they got into her tepee Little stick asked Tasillaqua, 'Refresh my memory how I got the name Little Stick?' and she revealed, 'Now that is a strange one. I recall our mother calling you Little Skye and you were a real skinny little kid and when you reached the age of four you got really curious about events in our village. But you were too small to push your way through the crowd in front of you because you weren't that strong and those little eyes lit up when you spotted a stick on the ground and you picked it up and started poking people in the legs out of your way. You even did it to our dad and he then remarked "well look who it is, Little Stick" and after that it stuck! So goodnight, sweet dreams!' and then they went to sleep.

The next morning they got up early and went with their dad for a ride on the Great Plains for a little hunting of anything they could find and it was a big mountain lion. Mutt went with them and after they hit the lion with a few well aimed arrows, he went in and brought him down and it was a good bonding day for the two girls and their dad. Then she rode over to the trading post and asked Senga, 'When is the next train due tomorrow?' and she remarked, 'Now that is a short visit,' and added, 'About two o'clock, so why the big rush?' 'I have something to discuss with William', she replied, 'It is something he never mentioned to me!' Senga asked her, 'Is it serious?' and she replied, 'It is to him but in a good way,' and on came that big smile again.

Then Senga said, 'I must pay you for the glasses you brought,' and she remarked, 'Oh don't worry about that, have them on me he would gladly swallow the cost,' and she asked, 'Are you sure?' and then on came that smile and she replied, 'Trust me I am an optimist!' Off she went back to the village and so all things were back to normal there and her mother couldn't keep from fussing over her and revealed, 'These new glasses really help me at sewing I no longer keep stabbing myself. You really are a clever girl,' and added, 'Have you eaten yet?' After Little Stick kissed her head she replied, 'Don't worry about me I am perfectly fine, I just wanted to sit here and take it all in. It is so lovely and peaceful here but I am really happy in the big city. There is a lot happening in there, some good and some not so good, but I can cope. I see Dad is still fighting fit as usual!' and her mum then remarked, 'He really likes your young white man and me too, so how is he? ' She replied, 'He is working hard in the shop but he is a touch shy of me,' and her mother remarked, 'That is a good sign,' and off she rode to the trading post and asked Senga, 'Can your boy take me to the railway after I change into my western clothes?' and she replied, 'Of course he can.' When they arrived at the track her sister told her, 'Just stand up and wave to the driver and he will stop for you,' and she did just that and to her amazement it stopped right there. Out came the guard and it was the same one she had on her incoming trip and he remarked, 'Ah the pretty lady once again,' and added, 'Now that was a quick visit.' He took her heavy bag on board and then he lifted her aboard and asked her, 'So how was it?' and she replied, 'Quite truly informative and it revealed to me the problem in my head was really nothing and life is all fine!'

The trip back was quite uneventful for her but the engine was needing some water quite frequently and it stopped a few times on the way to refill. But it got to New York central only thirty minutes late and when she got off she met that rude posh lady and she walked straight past her. But Little Stick wasn't having it and she called after her and asked her straight to her face, 'Remember me and my not so little dog!' and she went quite pink in the face and Little Stick then remarked, 'Remember, manners cost nothing, so I won't say anything rude to you now!' The lady just walked on without a whisper and Little Stick broke out with a big grin and thought to herself "now that makes me feel a lot better".

Now she didn't inform anyone that she was coming back early and it wasn't too long to walk to the shop. Then she realised it was Sunday morning, that the shop was closed and she didn't have a key because she was travelling overnight and never realised the time and that was six in the morning. She knew she had only one option left and that was to wake up Nicole in her room although she knew that she had maybe had a late night. So she thought "just how can I get in?" and she gathered some small pebbles from the street and started throwing them at her window on the second floor, not too hard. That did the trick and up came her window and out came Nicole's head and she shouted up at her, 'Let me in please I am back early,' and she replied, 'I will be down in a minute, must put something on first.' Then Mutt had a wee against a nearby lamppost and she said to him, 'Do you have to do that now?!' and when the door opened she rushed straight past Nicole and headed straight to the little girl's room. When she came out she addressed her good friend and said, 'Oh I really needed that, thank you for the speed you came downstairs' Nicole replied, 'No big deal I have been there also,' and then she asked her, 'So why back so early?' and then Little Stick revealed to her, 'Now I know his problem. He hasn't gone off me he is quite normal, nothing wrong with him. My dad told me he swore on his heart that he wouldn't touch me because of my age!' Nicole enquired, 'So just how old were you when you arrived in New York?' and she replied, 'Nearly fourteen,' and Nicole then exclaimed, 'You mean thirteen. My dad would hit the roof if it was me,' and then added, 'I thought you were a bit young when you arrived here but not that young!' Little Stick further explained, 'He just said to me when he put that light on I had the most beautiful eyes he had ever seen and he did not make any advances on me and I took that as the nicest compliment I ever got in my whole life and just then I was besotted with him after that remark. Do you think I am a silly little girl?' 'Not at all.' Nicole replied, 'I think you are a real smart little cookie,' and added, 'Well you do have nice eyes and I know they come with a real hot temper!' Little Stick gave a little smile and admitted, 'They really do! And William reckoned I spit fire when I get upset with someone.' Then Nicole asked her, 'So what will you do now?' and she replied, 'Oh I will just stroll in with you in the morning and then have a little chat with him that is all.' Nicole then asked her, 'Have you eaten yet?' and she replied, 'No, not for a long time,' and added, 'You sound just like my mother.' Nicole suggested, 'Good, let us go into the cafe now, have a bit of breakfast then a nice long walk in the sunshine and back into the cafe for a spot of lunch. They do a nice one every Sunday and maybe even a nice juicy bone for Mutt!' and Little Stick then asked her, 'Do I look all right?' and she scoffed back, 'Don't push your luck with me, little girly, you always look all right!' And off they went with Mutt right behind them.

In the cafe they both had a small breakfast and went on for a long walk and Mutt was a happy dog. But their walk took much longer than they planned and they didn't get back for lunch in time to meet the lads from the shop because they generally went in there at twelve o'clock. The waitress told them, 'They all left dead on one,' and added, 'So what will you have, girls?' and Little Stick said, 'Two roast beef dinners and a bone for my dog who is chained up outside!' She remarked, 'I have only one large bone at the moment,' and Little Stick replied, 'My dog is a large one so that would be fine.' Then she addressed Nicole and said, 'This one is on me so put your money away,' and outside Mutt was gnawing away quite noisily with no regard for the people near him and when they left he took it with him all the way back to his new home, always walking right behind them.

The next morning they headed to the shop and she paused at the doorway and said to Nicole, 'Please after you, they don't know I am back and don't say a word. Let me make my entrance. I will just breeze in. Just close the door after you,' and Nicole then remarked, 'Well you are not a shy one are you?' and she replied, 'Not in any way!' Then she opened the door slightly to let Mutt slide in and he ran straight to William just as she planned and his eyes were fixed on the dog at that given moment. Now it was her turn and she ran straight at him and gave him a kiss on his open mouth and he quickly shut it and then she gave him another one when he closed his mouth and he was truly stunned. She then said, 'Mister, I need a word with you!' and then it clicked in his head that she had found out and asked her, 'So now you know,' and she replied, 'I surely do! Why did you not tell me I nearly stayed back there until my dad told me about your given word. I nearly lost you forever you stupid boy!' Then she said, 'I am quite happy to stay with Nicole for the time being,' and his almost silent reply was just, 'Good!' All the rest of the staff just stood there and listened speechless and now it was almost time to open the shop. Mutt took his bone in there too and was chewing away on it quietly in the corner at the front door so Fred gave him a little shove out of the way with his leg and turned their sign to indicate they were open.

She then told Fred she was willing to work for the rest of the week although she had booked a whole week off and he remarked, 'Fine, would love to have you around,' and added, 'Is everything all right now?' and she replied, 'It is now!'

Chapter Eight

After a year and a half New York was booming and so was the shop's business but the shop next door wasn't doing so well. Its owner had a word with Fred and told him his business was losing lots of money and he asked Fred if he could buy him out. Fred remarked, 'Must consult my young associate, because he is the one who makes all the big money decisions!' and he said this because he knew young William was much better than him to haggle the best price for the property since he knew all the faults in the property to pick out to pull down the asking price. So he told the owner "let me think it over" and then he consulted William in the big room and asked him, 'What do you think of next door?' and he remarked, 'It would make a super living space for all of us and we could make a little passage through to the shop to it but we would need to get in a professional team to do that work!' Fred agreed to that and said to him, 'So we will buy it!' and he replied, 'Without question let us speak to him tomorrow morning,' and they did just that at precisely nine o'clock. The owner brought the price down by quite a few hundred dollars when William pointed out the leaking roof and the damp corners and so on and he agreed with his offer. They shook hands and William then told him, 'We will pay cash tomorrow in full,' and then Fred said to him, 'I knew you would come in useful on this trip that is why I told Mr Scarlet you are my chosen one regardless of your age and he readily agreed because he had great faith in you even though you were a street lad!'

About three weeks previously Roseanne had informed Fred that they were about to get one hefty tax bill this year because of the shop's successful year in trading and advised him to find a way to reduce this now. That is the main reason he bought the premises next door. Now Roseanne was the bookkeeper in the firm and also dealt with all the orders and general contracts and she was a key worker but kept herself to herself and she treated the shop's business the same way, which is exactly why he hired her. Now this premises next to the shop was itself a shop but not a successful one and it was about the same size on three floors and perfect for converting into the living space they needed. But Fred didn't want to attempt to do it themselves and he hired in some proper builders whilst William set about making the plans for the interior. He came up with three apartments on the ground floor and then two apartments on the top floor for the two girls along with one big lounge for staff meetings in the middle floor. He showed his plan to the team of builders they had hired and their boss man told him "We can do that", gave him a price and Fred told him, 'Agreed.' It took them about six months to complete the project and it was better than they imagined when they saw the finished result so now they had to furnish it top to bottom with no expense spared. After all, it was going to be their home for many years.

Now both girls weren't that keen at first when they heard that they were getting new living arrangements next to the shop because both valued their precious independence of a private space but when they saw the fittings and furniture moving in and were told it was rent free they quickly changed their minds. Fred then said to them, 'No peeking before it is finished,' and they didn't but he and William went in every other day just to check the progress. Eventually it was all done in time and Fred gave the builders the thumbs up and stated, 'Nice job, it is well worth it,' and paid the final balance to their boss and told him, 'Love it, just what the doctor had ordered.' The boss remarked, 'The biggest headache was ripping out all the old woodwork and cheap fittings but you are happy?' and he replied, 'Very.' Fred then gave William some money and said, 'Buy some decent alcohol, we must christen the place before we move in!' he took the note and replied, 'Will do' and bought quite a lot just in case they ran out. The next day they moved in and the two girls screamed with delight when they saw their separate apartments with fitted showers and a toilet for each of them. They rushed downstairs just to kiss Fred on the cheek – and William too of course – and then they all gathered in the big middle room for a big celebration which went on for a good part of that night.

The next week on there was another celebration as it was Little Stick's eighteenth birthday. She had no idea that they had planned a little party for her as they had done it all on the quiet and so Nicole led her into the big room with her hands firmly clasped over her eyes and then asked her to remove them. She let out a mighty scream of delight and uttered to her, 'I forgot all about it,' and then she added, 'I suppose this was your idea!' and she replied, 'Not me, honey, but William's, he planned this weeks ago.' Then in came the rest of the staff and some from their little cafe bringing a big cake and other goodies and down came the tears but she quickly wiped them away and started kissing everyone nearest to her. She left William right to the end and he gave her one enormous cuddle but he was quite unsure just where to place his hands after that, and she told him, 'Just go for it I am no longer a little girl.' Still he hesitated because he had never had a girl that close to him in the past, nor had she had a man this close and she was dead keen to discover this new pleasure. But then he made a feeble excuse and said to her, 'Not in front of all of these people,' and then he broke off the embrace to her displeasure. Then he said, 'I bought you a sweet little ring for your birthday it is in my pocket let me show you,' and he took it out and said, 'It used to belong to a princess in Burma, a faraway land from here,' and he then slipped it on to her finger. 'I love it!' she remarked and added, 'It is not a betrothed ring is it? Because I wouldn't like you to own me. I love to be independent!' and he then remarked lightly, 'Don't be silly, that is much too scary for me. It is just a friendship ring from me to you!' She laconically replied, 'Good,' and left it on her finger and gave him a little kiss on his cheek The party around them was getting a bit lively to say the least because the drink was flowing and the food on the table was

71

diminishing rather quickly so they both grabbed something to eat before it was all gone and the party was over.

Upstairs in their new apartments both girls admired their fittings and Nicole remarked in her room, 'Now this is not too bad,' and Little Stick remarked back to her, 'Not too bad, this is sheer luxury compared to your little room,' and gave a small laugh and asked her, 'Just how much would this cost if you had to rent it?' Nicole replied, 'About half of our wages I suppose and we don't even have to walk to our shop,' and added, 'I just love working for the English,' and Little Stick stated, 'Me too!' Just then the alcohol she had consumed that night suddenly hit her fully, and she felt her way back into her own apartment and just about made it to her bed even though she was still fully dressed. The next morning she sprung out of it, got changed into fresh clothes and went down to the cafe with Nicole to have a coffee and some toast before getting into the shop bang on time at eight. She said to herself, "Never again will I drink too much alcohol in such a short space of time," and added out loud, 'But then again it was such a lovely night.' Now William was delighted with this new living arrangement because he could see her more often but Fred had other plans for him and he told him flatly, 'Young man we have a lot more work on our plate this coming year and that means spending more time in the workshop at night so don't think these new premises will give you more time to court that young lady. I didn't do it for you but for the business because we have a whopping great tax demand this year and the outlay for our new property will bring that bill down quite a lot. I have made a mathematical calculation on it and we will benefit quite a lot from it money-wise so it is time to get your head down and make it pay out even more. So put your passions on the back burner for a little while longer and that is final okay!' William then realised that she was in his head most of his time and that would not help to further his progress in the firm and he then replied swiftly, 'Okay, Fred, will do.' Now that threw some water on their forthcoming romance and it also gave him a little more time to think about the best way to approach her because as he well knew sometimes she is hot and sometimes she is icy cold but the best thing about their new living space is they can always meet in the 'halfway room' as she named it.

It was fully fitted out with a large table and a good seating area along with a drinks bar and even a nice log fire for those winter nights. Just downstairs all three men had their own private apartments and all of them led to a massive front door in the place where the previous shop's window had been. It was made out of solid hardwood and this was locked every night at precisely one o clock for safety. One more little treasure was a small corridor between the shop and the ground floor of these apartments which was purely for the convenience of the men only, so that they didn't have to open the main door to retrieve something they had forgotten. The girls who lived upstairs knew nothing about it because they would never have to use it. This conversion of the premises cost about the same price as the shop itself but Fred and William were very happy with the total cost of their purchase. Tim was quite a loner and took no interest in the business side of the shop but he was an excellent worker on the frames and that is why Fred took him along too. Now Roseanne didn't move in because she had a husband and two kids in a sweet little apartment not too far away and she was a lady much older than the other two girls and only took the position to help support her own household. She was always on time and always left at the same time to pick up her kids from school and Fred once remarked, 'You could set your watch by her,' and thought she was a nice steady lady just what our little team needs. Now and again he would wire the firm back in London to inform their progress to keep the old man up to date but he never gave him any information about William's forthcoming romance because in his eyes there was simply nothing to tell of great interest.

Another year had passed and the city had grown even bigger and so had the shop's business and they carried on turning out their popular eye glasses. So come one Sunday over lunch Little Stick knew that William was hard at work along with the other two and she asked him, 'Take me out for something completely different like in town for maybe a show or a spot of dinner because I am so fed up sitting in my apartment all alone. Nicole isn't always there as she is always out every other night but I have nowhere to go!' To that request William put on a sad face and said, 'Aww you poor thing let us go to a little pub not too far away from the shop. No need to dress up just go in your casual clothes you will enjoy it. A nice little Irish pub that I used to visit when we first came here. There is nice simple food, singing and dancing and not one snooty person in sight,' and she responded with glee, 'Let us go there tonight.' But first he said, 'Must take Mutt for his little walk first into the park and beyond.' Now the thrill of actually going out in the evening with him really got to her and he had been looking for a chance to actually ask her out but now there was no need for that. He was thrilled to bits when she asked him to take her out and just before they left she told Mutt in a very firm voice, 'Stay right there!' and he nearly nodded in agreement. 'So how come he always does everything you say?' he asked her and she replied, 'An old Indian trick. There are lots of them,' and he remarked, 'I bet there are,' and off they went hand in hand down the street. It was still quite light and they walked into this sweet little pub.

She just loved the whole atmosphere and the people within and the barman said to William, 'Hello stranger, long time no see. So who is this pretty lady with you?' and he replied, 'Oh just someone from the shop.' Then he kissed her forehead and the barman remarked, 'I think otherwise. She is much too pretty to work in a shop.' Then the band started up, but not too loud, and he told him, 'Your favourite is on the menu tonight, a nice roasted venison.' So William ordered, 'Two please and some light beers and we would like a nice quiet corner table.' The barman replied, 'We have the table but I don't promise you it will be quiet, not on Sunday evening,' and Little Stick then remarked, 'There are real people in here. I love it. New York let your hair down!' and added, 'I never knew many white people before and I thought they were all quite grumpy but now after this night I think a little differently. Thank you William for opening my eyes. You really are quite a sweetheart.'

Then the band stopped playing and the fiddle player announced, 'If there are any singers out there who are keen to sing with our little band?' and Little Stick shot up her hand and called, 'Me me!' William enquired, 'I didn't know you could sing!' and she retorted, 'I have many talents that you don't know about. For instance my skill with a skinning knife, I got my first feather for that at the age of twelve,' and he stated, 'I do know that one. Remember I watched you skinning that animal on the plains.' Then she turned to the fiddle player and asked, 'Can I keep my hat on?' and he replied, 'Absolutely just go for it!' and then she told him, 'It is in the key of C, slowly but gently,' and added, 'Just let me catch my breath.' She did that quite deliberately and out came a powerful, 'Amazing Grace' and this little band wasn't quite ready for that. She had done this purely for effect and the slick little band slid into it smoothly when she got to the verse, and the whole crowd in there gave her a mighty round of applause when she finished the song and they asked for more. 'Okay,' she said, 'this is one of my true favourite songs; it's called Over the Hills and Far Away,' and the band was stunned with her delivery and asked her to sing a few more. 'Maybe next week,' she stated as she headed back to her table and William was truly amazed and asked her, 'Where did that come from?' She smiled and replied, 'Maybe from that good old fresh air back in Oklahoma,' and added, 'I feel a touch tingly now but not when I was singing up there.'

They stayed there right to the end of the show and then over came two of the band members and sat down beside their table and the fiddle player asked her directly, 'Would you like a position in our band? We really need a front line singer, someone like you.' She responded, 'I have already got a good position in a shop but I would certainly sing with you on another Sunday night if you would let me!' and he remarked, 'Let you! we would be very happy if you would do that every Sunday!' He turned to William and asked him, 'So what do you think?' and he replied, 'Well it is her life I don't interfere in that. She has a mind of her own, she is a free spirit!' That last remark prompted her to say, 'I will do every Sunday with your little band with the greatest pleasure, but let me ponder on the rest!'

When they went back home she went into his apartment and asked him, 'Can you teach me to play the guitar just a little, nothing too fancy please. I have observed that you have two of them so you must have some idea about them?' and he remarked, 'I am no teacher but I can show you a few chords and a few little fancy licks but nothing too clever,' and she said, 'That will do nicely.' They started that the following evening just after they shut up the shop. Now all that constant overtime had come to a stop upstairs in their workshop and he was now free in the evenings so he allowed her just one hour of his time to pursue her latest venture. But when he saw her progress in the first session with her nimble fingers and her sheer will to succeed to get it right, he then pushed even further until she complained that her fingers were in pain. That was after three hard hours at it and now she needed a little cuddle and he did not refuse and this made her very pleased. Up she went into her apartment and rubbed some cream into her hands and William thought "she has got something planned in the future for certain about this singing career" and he was spot on. Over the next few nights, she was really going for it trying out new rhythms and always asking him for some little tricks about playing the instrument and he gladly gave her some suggestions for instance hitting the strings with her hand rather than playing it normally and this she picked up quite naturally because being an Indian, drums were in her nature. Then she asked him, 'Can I borrow this guitar to use next Sunday?' and he frankly told her, 'It is much too soon for that!' and added, 'Maybe give it another few weeks.' Again she asked him for a quick cuddle before she left and of course he didn't refuse.

Now during her working day she still gave it her full commitment attending to old and young clients because that was her chosen profession and it kept a roof over her head. William was always close by and slowly, slowly, he became more affectionate towards her because he no longer thought she was just a young girl but he wouldn't dare try anything outlandish towards her for the simple fact that he just didn't know how to approach it. But he was quite contented about her guitar lessons just because he was close to her and the thought that she just might take it a little too seriously about playing in this band full time did cross his mind. That could become quite a blow to his dedication to the shop he had helped to establish in this new country but that was something he might have to contend with in the future and not right now, because everything was sailing quite smoothly at the moment.

Now he stepped up her nightly lesson from one hour to three hours with a ten minutes break in between and she coped rather well with this pace and on Saturday evening he took her out on the town just for a little treat for all that effort she put in during her lessons. The following Sunday, he planned to take her on a special trip to somewhere she had never been and that was Niagara Falls. Why? Because he wanted to distract her from her singing ambitions and set her mind on the shop, which was his project and he was determined to make it a total success. When she arrived there, she gasped with delight and asked him, 'Can we go underneath it?' and he replied, 'Why not,' and he asked one of the men, 'Can we go on a boat ride in it?' and he remarked, 'You can but you will come out soaked to the skin!' 'Fine by me,' she replied, 'let us do it,' and in they went. It was quite a big boat and they supplied them with raincoats and she thought it was quite fun. After drying out, he took her for a nice lunch and then a long walk in the park. Then they went straight to the pub and up to the stage she went, and her first song was Swing Low Sweet Chariot and the little band let her sing the first four bars. Then in they came with the full melody and she sang this up beat but with a low tone. The crowd listened in silence at first, then they all joined in and called out for more and by now she was up to scratch with all of their songs and did a few more. Then the girl guitarist sang a few and the fiddle player, then back once more to Little Stick. William just sat at his table and grinned at her performance on stage and she stayed there the whole evening. When it was all over two of the band came over to him at his table and said 'we would love to have her in the band' and he just shrugged his shoulders and replied, 'It is not up to me ask her. she is a free woman!' Little Stick wasn't too sure this second time about the free woman statement bit or his general reaction and explained to him, 'It is only local and nearby performances I will do!' He remarked, 'Fine by me but remember you have your position in the shop. Do not let that go!' and she answered, 'Don't you approve?' and he replied, 'You pick your own path in life just like I pick mine, so it is entirely up to you!' She turned to the fiddle player and said, 'Okay I am in but on one condition. You will pay me nightly!' and he replied, 'Agreed.'

On their way back home he was almost silent but then she took his hand and swung it a little and enquired, 'What do you think?' and he almost grunted a reply and said, 'It has nothing to do with me. It is your future not mine!' That answer didn't go down too well with her but in his head he thought he might be losing her. Although of course he never said it. Back home all the rest were chilling out in the big room with a little drink before they settled down and he and she took Mutt out for his nightly stroll. They were actually holding hands when they walked because in front of the rest of staff that was not looked upon as being proper. Fred laid down the rules and he was into old school's rules and that didn't go down well with her but she knew that if she broke them it meant she was out of the door and would lose everything, even William, so she kept her mouth firmly shut.

Now, this new stage in her life wouldn't start straight away because she must learn the band's whole routine to perfection and the fiddle player told her, 'You have got four weeks before you start so have some time off and try to get it right and after that we will move into larger venues and that is when you can expand your skills as a front singer and make a big impression and a lot more money.' This she agreed without any dispute and William then thought this over and stated to her, 'You must tell Fred about this, and your dad back home.' She nearly brushed this off then she answered, 'I will,' but that wasn't the end of it as she found out later. William then asked Fred on the following Monday, 'We both need a trip to Oklahoma for about ten days just to clear some things up!' and he replied, 'Okay just for a little break to clear things up, that's fine by me.' That was one part of the situation fixed, but life is never that simple. He told Little Stick they were going there and it was almost fall time and her nineteenth birthday, so he bought her some new warmer clothes. This time he picked them out – a set of good hard wearing denims, a nice warm check shirt and a big hat followed by a long leather coat and she asked him, 'Can you afford it?' He replied, 'I don't want you shivering in that breezy weather and I must work a bit more at night, so no big problem and I will also wire the town nearest to the trading post so that they can pick us up from the train.'

Chapter Nine

That big day arrived, and their train was due to leave at six in the evening. A problem arose because he asked her, 'What will we do about the dog?' and she replied in a fickle manner, 'We will just take the old boy with us. He is free to take on board.' He agreed to that and slipped his chain on, looked him straight in the face and said, 'Ready for a long trip!' and Mutt almost nodded in agreement. On they went and luckily for her it was the same chatty guard who let them on the first time. He addressed her first and enquired, 'So this is that lucky young man who captured your heart?' and William just gave him a little nod in greeting. Then he asked her, 'Is it all the way to Oklahoma again?' She replied, 'Just to have a little chat with my family but really to have my father's approval,' and he remarked back, 'No problem with him he is a fine looking fellow!' Then William asked him, 'So where do we sit?' and the guard replied, 'With that dog we will put you right at the end as before.' He then turned to her and stated, 'You know where to go,' and they settled themselves in their seats and got organised with their bits and pieces at last.

Now Little Stick had thought well ahead of this little surprise trip to good old Oklahoma because just before they left she got everything they needed on their journey. She popped into the cafe and bought some food and wine for their trip and she produced it to his amazement and he said to her, 'Now you're truly someone really special.' So they had a little feast on their way there and after that they wrapped themselves in their blankets and it was a night full of cuddles. They woke up at the same time fresh as a daisy as their day to alight arrived and then the guard called out, 'Next stop after this one is the Cherokee Nation so get ready to alight!' Then he glanced out of the window and said to them, 'There are two wagons waiting there,' and the driver slowed to a stop and they got out with a little help from the guard and everyone in the wagons was waving at them. William then thought "now that is a good sign" and he asked her, 'So where is your dad?' and she replied, 'Coming up on his horse just left on the wagons.' He remarked, 'He looks mighty fine on his horse don't you think so!' and she gave a little nod to confirm and said, 'I reckon so,' and then her mother cried out from the wagon, 'Now what have they done to my little baby they have turned her into a man!' Tasillaqua who was sitting right next to her said, 'She is only wearing practical western clothing to keep the cold out of her bones so, don't worry, she is still your little girl although she is looking a lot bigger and even more prettier. Just how does she do it!' Then Little Stick jumped straight into the wagon and gave them both a big hug and William climbed in after her and Mutt was quite happy to trot alongside on to the trading post. Senga was standing outside to greet them and she said, 'That city life suits you well, you look amazing. So how are things in the big city?'

She replied, 'William makes me really happy and keeps me very busy in the shop and I just love it in New York but it is always nice to come back here to see you all,' and added, 'So how is business?' and Senga remarked, 'Oh so-so but I do need some of those eyeglasses. They are very popular among the old gents in the nearby towns.' Little Stick revealed to her, 'He has brought two whole cases just for you. Isn't that sweet of him and he is only putting a small profit on them just over the cost price, does that suit you?' and Senga remarked, 'Not half. I can make a fine profit on them and they will fly out of the door!' Then she asked Little Stick, 'So where are you living now, not with him?' and she replied, 'No no, we all have separate apartments in the same building. I know that might sound strange but his boss is a real business man and he had figured out if he bought the shop next door which was up for sale and turned it into living space for his workers then he could claim that cost against his tax demand for that year. Up to then all three men slept in a tiny room above the shop. I know nothing about tax demands – it is just way out of my league – but he did it and so he paid less tax for the shop's profits that year and all the apartments are fully fitted out with things you wouldn't have dreamed of!' Her dad was still sitting on his horse when William approached him and he leaned over its neck and asked him straight out, 'Well is she still intact?' William replied, 'Absolutely I gave you my word!' Then he leapt off his horse, took his hand and gave it a strong shake and stated, 'At last a white man I can trust, now you can have her if it is still her wish!'

William felt quite embarrassed at this relevant, if surprising, remark but he gave no answer just a little cough to clear his dry throat and he just left it there.

Everyone else were now in the trading post and a few more people turned up so it wasn't quite a party, but nearly, and Senga was quite busy behind her counter selling bits and pieces at random. Then he placed the big case, which was full of little goodies he brought, firmly on the counter and started pulling a few out to reveal to all what was in there and gave Senga the cases that contained the eyeglasses. Now her big sister pulled her to one side and asked Little Stick, 'Just how do you do it? I am nearly as pretty as you are. It surely must be all that information stored in your little head and William told me it is your eyes that captured him first and the rest happened later?' Little Stick broke in just there and said to her, 'He gave me something I had never got before – a big compliment for no reason and no gain and I just loved that so I thought "let's just help him out for a while on the trail". He was chatty and funny but also a little serious and then it happened, I just couldn't get him out of my head and he told me I would make a good sales lady in the big city and I asked dad if I could go with him to there and he gave me the okay!' Tasillaqua remarked, 'So that is how it happens!' and she replied, 'Yep it sure does, just grab the bull by its horns and don't let go whatever happens.' Then they all headed to their village on the two wagons and her dad was out in front on his horse. William rode silently all the way because it was his party. In they went and he didn't feel in control any more which did worry him a little because he sensed there was something in the air.

There were drums bashing, horns blowing, kids screaming and some young braves staring at him in a not too friendly way, but he put it all down to Little Stick's arrival. He was spot on, because it was a giving away ceremony. But he didn't know that because no one had told him that he would have to fight for his girl against every young buck that challenged him on that day. Little Stick had completely forgotten about this ritual and then she thought "surely it doesn't apply to a white man" but it did. She asked Tasillaqua, 'Is this for real?' and she answered, 'You bet it is, there are three out there just dying to even touch you and would love to make you their squaw,' and she added, 'So how good is he with a knife or a tomahawk or a good old wrestle?' Little Stick replied worriedly, 'I don't really know! but he is pretty good with a pistol,' and Tasillaqua said, 'They don't allow guns. It must be face to face and hand to hand stuff!' 'He is fairly good at boxing – you know that hand to hand fighting in a little square that white men do!' she revealed and Tasillaqua remarked, 'Now that might just pass, okay we will go with that!' She told her dad and he passed it on to the elders and told them, 'No weapons just bare hands,' and they accepted that with no question.

Now William was still completely in the dark until Little Stick told him to remove his shirt and it clicked in his brain he was going to fight or catch a good suntan and when he did, all the young maidens standing there went, 'Woooo!' Yes, he had muscles and a very trim waist and he could use them from when he used to be a street fighter back in London in the east end. Tasillaqua was well impressed with that and one of his challengers just walked away after one glance at his body and he was the lucky one. Then the three men stood before the elders to get the rules of the contest. They were pretty basic: no weapons, no biting and no eye gouging but feet and head can be used. "So boys, let us get on with it and the victor will have the maiden."

So on went the first two standing toe to toe. William flicked a few punches to his head but that wasn't quite enough to put this big lad down who then gripped his arm and threw him in the dust and then sat on him. But William had enough power to move him off, although it wasn't easy, and did a little fancy footwork around him and went I with five punches to his gut. The lad staggered, a little unsteady on his feet and down he went with no chance of recovery. William then headed to his corner where the two girls were there to rub him down ready for his next opponent. Tasillaqua asked him, 'Does it hurt a lot?' and he remarked, 'What do you think? He has got a grip like an old croc he just doesn't let go!' and Little Stick stated, 'Please don't lose the next one, I would hate to end up in his tepee – and try to keep that face just the way I like it!' William had got just ten minutes to prepare to meet the next one and he was a champion wrestler in the village with a lot of weight to throw at him. In they went to the middle and he had no time to catch a second breath because this one threw himself straight at him when he reached the spot but he quickly dodged out of the way and danced around the back of him. But his present opponent had studied his every move in the first contest and he wouldn't fall into his way of fighting and in he came with another mighty rush and knocked him clean over. But William recovered himself quickly, brushed off the dust and threw four punches in his face and that made him a touch groggy. He was still up for it though and in he came again but this time he gripped both arms around William's whole body from the back then turned him over and sat on him and William was truly trapped in his grip. He took three quick gasps of air, lifted his head and gave him a severe butt on the nose and he immediately released his grip and wiped his bloody face. William then stood up, walked over to the sitting elders and stated, 'I think the maiden is mine!'

Now during that whole fight scene Mutt had been straining to get in there to save his master but both Little Stick and Tasillaqua were holding on grimly to his choker chain with both hands and when they saw him get up they let go just a little and gave him a meat bone and she patted his head and looked him straight in his face, 'Okay it is all over now calm down.' Tasillaqua remarked, 'Now that was a close one you nearly got big bad Jonn for keeps. Aren't you the lucky one!' Little Stick replied smugly, 'I knew he would not give me up for someone like him or for anyone else because he is real sweet on me,' and her big sister remarked back, 'Don't be too cocky in the future someone might just snap him away from you!' But she blanked this comment from her head and said, 'Now it is party time. I have brought a few bottles of wine from the big city so let us celebrate my warrior!' Just then he came over and told them, 'It hurts all over. Why didn't you tell me before?' and she then put on a sad face and replied, 'I didn't even know about that.'

So after that was all over, everyone was getting ready for the night's big event and there were cooking pots on the go outside almost every tepee. Both girls went into Tasillaqua's own tepee to sort out who was sleeping where but William had already made an arrangement with Senga that he could live in the trading post for his stay there for a small fee and that meant that he didn't break any of the rules of tradition. Whilst Little Stick said, 'Fine by me' and it went down really well with her dad it didn't really suit her and so she cut their stay there down to two days. Now that wasn't really a problem for him because he was the restless type always wanting to move on to new and exciting things. So when she revealed to him that she wasn't too happy to stay the whole week, he took it in his stride and very calmly replied, 'Whatever you wish I will do.' Then she casually mentioned, 'Mutt has taken quite a liking to Tasillaqua, can she keep him here? He has a lot more room to run around. I will miss him but he is getting too old and he needs the freedom to run free – can she?' That request gave him pause for thought and he stroked his chin a few times and said, 'Yes a good idea,' and added, 'But you must tell him in that special way that you are only doing it for him when you pat his head!' and she quickly replied, 'Okay will do, thanks.' He pondered a little and thought "just what is she up to on this cool and pleasant day".

Then it is off to that big night event and it was loud and noisy but nice and he even spoke to his two opponents. There were no hard feelings between them, only a little touch of jealousy, but they got on well enough thanks to the beer he brought with him. After it was all over they hit the sack and once again she slept with her big sister and she revealed to her, 'If someone had told me I would end up with a white man I would have laughed my silly head off' Tasillaqua replied, 'Now you always were a strange one even as a kid so nothing you do surprises me. Good night sweet dreams. I am shattered!' Over in the trading post Senga had set up a little sleeping part in her spare room just for him and he slept like a baby. The next morning he gave out all the gifts he had brought, along with the silver dollars for her dad and he was real happy for that and told his little baby, 'You have a good one there but just do not mess it up with your funny little ways.' 'I won't!' she retorted.

For the rest of that day, she borrowed two horses and took him to see the rest of the country around. He wasn't too impressed with this as he just wanted to go back home to New York but he didn't tell her. The next day they caught their train back home and both he and she breathed a huge sigh of relief. Their train arrived at the stop a touch late due to something on the line but they didn't care about that as they thought it was a pure pleasure to be going back to the big city. After the train shuddered to a halt, they threw their bags on the carriage first and then he lifted her in.

Luckily for him she was not that heavy because from the ground to the carriage it was quite a distance and once again she breathed a sigh of relief to be in his strong arms. Up came that big smile and then she revealed the food that his sister had prepared for their journey. It was quite a feast so after they'd eaten it they settled down under their blankets for the rest of their trip and she was a real happy girl.

Chapter Ten

At the end of their journey the train pulled into the station and they rushed to prepare to get ready for their departure and alight from the train. She then arranged herself to look proper and dipped into the small valise she was carrying, withdrew a small bag of gold and giving it to him said, 'This is from my dad in exchange for your dollars you gave to him.' Then she added, 'By the way, the elders made you a full Cherokee brother and that is quite a distinction for a white man!' He made no comment about that honour and she got off first. She had to avoid a lady standing right in her path and it was the rude lady she had confronted before and the lady stood there with a defiant glare on her face and she asked her, 'So where is the big bad wolf now?' Little Stick replied through her teeth with a blank stare, 'I left him back in my village,' and she scoffed back, 'Pity because those two men over there with my husband would like to chain him up and take him to the pound!' 'Over my dead body!' replied Little Stick and the rude lady nonchalantly replied with a grimace, 'Fine we will do it that way, you filthy Indian!' At that moment William appeared on the scene and asked quietly, 'So what is the problem here?' and the rude lady then remarked loudly and venomously, 'This little piece of trash threatened me with a dangerous dog some time ago and I want to get it put down.' He asked her politely, 'So what is your position in society. Are you up there in power or just an ordinary citizen like me or this young lady?' Little Stick didn't say a single word through this whole scene and then along came her husband with two men carrying a net and chains to catch the wild dog who wasn't there. William then produced a pencil and a little notebook and asked her husband, 'So what is this about?' and he replied snappily, 'I am a member of the senate on the democrat side of the house!' He then admitted he didn't really know what was going on but then revealed his own views that all Indians were underdogs and he had no idea that they had their own rights to live in this vast country. William pencilled this all down and he then threw all this back in his face and remarked, 'Now that is not very democratic surely to bully a young native American girl?' and added, 'You should be ashamed of yourself and of your party. I will go public with this in every newspaper in the country and I would crush the likes of you into the ground where you belong!'

After that remark the man got a bit twitchy and started to shuffle his feet and when William and the young girl walked away and his wife finally opened her mouth out came a stream of expletives on the subject and she exclaimed, 'How dare anyone speak to you in that manner about democratic affairs and you just stood there and said almost nothing in return. I will sue him on your behalf for slander!' But he replied nervously, 'Please don't do that. I am up for re-election in a few months and if that hits the papers

I would be finished. Just leave it be.' Then she thought about the luxurious life she enjoyed at the moment which she wouldn't have any longer if that whole scene was printed in black and white in the press and he lost his seat in the house. So she gave it further thought and decided to drop the matter because that young man might just be a keen smooth sneaky reporter looking for some kind of scandal.

Meanwhile on their walk back home, Little Stick remarked, 'You didn't even look at me. You went straight to him and what a lecture you gave, I was truly impressed!' He then explained to her, 'If you have to have an extreme discourse with someone you first need to know where he stands and where are his weak points – and if you know that you are in control. It is called "sizing up" and it is basically a fight with words!' 'That is quite a brain you have in your head' she remarked, 'I am even more impressed by my personal warrior thank you for that!' and up came that big smile. Then she added, 'It is only six thirty. Just come straight back to my place, nobody knows we are back,' and he replied, 'They will as soon as we open that big front door. Remember, we all live in the same place now?' 'Oh I forgot about that,' she said and he stated with a grin, 'They are probably all up and getting ready for the day, let's just drop off the bags and go for breakfast instead,' and she gave him a quick salute and said snappily, 'Yes sir!' Then he swung open the big door and called to Fred, 'It is only me back early just dropping off my cases and then we are off to get some breakfast!'

Luckily for them the cafe opened every morning

dead on six and so the griddle was hot and the coffee was already on and they both had eggs and bacon with fried tomatoes and lots of toast because both of them were really hungry after that long journey. Some time later the other three came in to catch up on their recent trip into the west and Fred then enquired, 'So what are you going to do in the next four days because you surely do not want to work in the shop?' William just sat there with a blank look waiting for the punchline and out it came. 'How about a little trip to Canada?' Fred said, 'We have got a big order from Quebec from a camp of Indians and want someone to go out there and test some eyes. Would you like to take it on?' William did not reply. Back in the shop Fred showed William the wire he received and he quickly glanced over it and Little Stick then broke into his thoughts and said, 'Oh yes we will take it on!' and added 'which tribe is it?' Nicole revealed, 'It is from that catalogue we advertised to the trading posts, so that is money well spent. It is from the Huron tribe in Quebec and it said "wire me back if you can see us on site!"' Little Stick quickly whipped the paper out of her hand and stated, 'They speak Iroquois. No big problem, me too,' and then she turned to William and asked him, 'Are you up for it?' and he just gave her a quick nod because he knew there was no point doing anything else. So it was decided that both of them would go to Quebec to meet new people and especially native Americans from the old days but he was a bit nonplussed about this unexpected new venture into Canada and he thought "well I suppose it is good for the shop's turnover".

So he planned this trip to the north with precision and took all they needed to make it advantageous for the shop. He even packed a few things he had never brought before on any previous trips and his two big bags were full and heavy which didn't really bother him because he was a fatalist and he believed what would be would be. So up came the big day when they were leaving for Canada at precisely nine in the morning and so they finished off their breakfast fairly swiftly and took a horse drawn carriage to the station and he checked in with great haste and booked a row of seats just for them with room to spread out if it was required. Off they went into the north, headed towards Quebec. It was a really sunny day but a bit nippy outside and Little Stick remarked, 'I just love your choo choo train it makes me feel as free as a bird!' and added, 'Does that sound silly to you?' He politely replied, 'Nothing you say will sound silly to me I just adore you for yourself,' and that brought on that big smile. Then she asked him, 'So how long to Quebec?' and he said, 'I reckon around six or seven hours so no time to sleep, let's just sit back and enjoy the view,' which they did for most of the way in between small chats and a few odd questions that he didn't know the answers to. The train pulled into their station and they stepped off and there waiting for them was a wagon with two mature men and one said, 'Hi, I am Hanuka, thanks for coming all this way on behalf of my people!' and Little Stick remarked, 'You speak English. I thought I would have to translate every word you said!' 'No need for that,' he replied, 'we have a school here that teaches us

English!' and he added, 'You are a native?' and she proudly replied, 'I am a full Cherokee from Oklahoma!' After this they both had a chat in their native language followed by a little giggle by her. And William was none the wiser.

The camp was quite a big one with not one single tepee in sight and they rolled up to the biggest wooden barn – or maybe it was a meeting place for the people – and in it were gathered many people who were in need of their skill and even a few white people who were informed that they were coming to test eyes. Right in the middle of the room was a massive table to set up their instruments, all well thought out William was pleased to observe, so they commenced testing – she at one side and he at the other. They split them up into two separate lines just to make it flow smoother and they also recruited one young lady to write down the readings they called out against their proper names. She did a remarkable job for a first timer because Little Stick had pulled her aside before the testing began and gave her all the correct forms along with a handful of pencils. So they finished the two lines just before ten in the evening, packed up all their instruments and were just ready to leave when Hanuka insisted they must stay overnight because his people would like to thank you for your presence and your time and he added, 'I would like to know you better!'

At this Little Stick stubbornly dropped her bag to the floor and announced, 'Fine suits me,' but William was not so keen and said, 'Okay no rush but where will we stay?' The young girl they recruited to do the paperwork said, 'You can have my cabin it is small but cosy and warm. It will suit you fine and I can move into my parent's place. Please do.' He didn't refuse the graceful offer and he took her hand and kissed it, so they stayed there the night and slept well throughout that chilly evening. The camp threw a little welcoming party for them later that night and presented her with a smart handmade beaver coat and a matching hat and they also gifted him a bigger hat. The party lasted well into the night. Next morning they got up with the rising sun and some of the women in the tribe were up already to prepare their breakfast and take them back to the station. Chief Hanuka told him, 'We don't have any American dollars. Will gold nuggets do?' and he replied, 'Fine by me!' and added, 'They will be ready in about eight days. It is quite a big order so it will take some time to prepare,' and added, 'My shop will wire you to let you know when it is to arrive.' Little Stick then donned her new coat and hat for the journey back home and remarked to him, 'Really nice friendly people. I bet we do a lot more business with them.'

The train trip back home was quite uneventful but the view out of the window was quite amazing for her and she adored her new coat and remarked, 'It is nice and cuddly, just like you,' and he wryly remarked back, 'So now I have a rival. That is strange coming from you, I thought I was the best. 'Oh you know what I mean!' she snapped back at him. Their train pulled into New York station and after one brief look around he saw there no carriages available, so he decided to walk all the way home while lugging both cases. They strolled down there at a leisurely pace due to their weight and nearly every lady who passed them by took a glance at her fine coat and a few actually stopped for a closer look and asked her, 'Where did you buy it?' and with a smug look she replied, 'Oh it is a gift from some of my clients in Canada. We have just been there. It is really soft, you can stroke it if you like.' Some of them actually did and that made her smile.

Then into the shop they went and she opened the door for a now exhausted William and let him through first and asked Tim, 'Give that poor soul a hand with the cases. We walked all the way back because there were no carriages available, he really needs a rest the poor thing,' and added, 'My true warrior. He never gives up!' Then Nicole rushed towards her and said, 'Give me a cuddle. I think it is rich. You look amazing. Gosh it is so soft and it suits your happy little face.' Fred then came downstairs and exclaimed, 'Well, I suppose it was a good trip looking at her but you, boy, look like a wreck. You just never give up do you and that is exactly why I brought you here. Go down to the cafe and refuel yourself right now. We will talk later.'

After he had refreshed himself, William came back into the premises along with Little Stick and while she withdrew the precious paperwork, he took the small bag of gold nuggets out of his inside pocket and handed it to Fred who remarked, 'Good work,' and added, 'No hassle, no problems?' William replied, 'Not one. Very nice friendly people. Big camp, very organised and they adored her and that coat was a gift for her excellent attention she gave to the people. I gave an eight days delivery on one hundred and fifty-seven pairs so we have to work quite a lot of overtime from now to then!' Fred remarked, 'Fine we will do that no problem, even through the night. Are you up for that?' and William replied, 'First let me finish the remainder of my holiday. I have two days left and I would like it to be something that she will never forget!' Fred then suggested, 'Take her to Washington DC to see the President. He has a little walk in the park nearly every Saturday to make an announcement to the people. She would love to see the "big white man's chief" as she would call him!' 'Great idea,' said William, 'we will go there, thanks,' and Fred gave him some details of a hotel he had stayed at when he went there and told him they are very strict on security because this hotel was pretty near the White House, so tell her be on best behaviour.' 'Will do,' replied William. Tomorrow was Friday, so he dashed up to the station first thing in the morning and booked the tickets to make sure they got a seat that day there and back. Over breakfast, he broke the news to Little Stick about their surprise trip to the White House to see their big white chief and she was simply thrilled to bits at this. Little Stick asked him, 'Can I wear my new coat there?' and he thought "now that is a strange question", but of course he knew absolutely nothing about the way girls think and he replied, 'Sure why not, it looks great on you and it will keep you nice and warm.'

Chapter Eleven

The morning promised a nice cloud-free sunny day and as they headed to the station in came their train full of mainly business people and they settled down for the journey there. Sitting down a few rows away from them Little Stick had spotted that rude lady sitting with her husband but she hadn't noticed her and she then cuddled close to William, pulled her hat down further over her eyes and just sat there contented as a flea in a rug. As the train pulled into Washington DC and almost everyone got off, she made sure to keep a safe distance away from that rude lady. When they arrived at the White House lawns for a little stroll it was packed full of people of all sorts and now, she was on guard more than usual and she scanned the crowd carefully one by one. She spotted quite a few that she didn't like the look of, but then thought what a pleasant way to spend the day in these posh gardens. Suddenly the President himself came out for a quick walkabout and made a short speech for the people.

It was Mr President Ulysses S Grant in person surrounded by at least twelve armed men just in case someone would try to take him out with a well-aimed shot and William told Little Stick, 'Now there is a man who runs the whole country and he is on the Indians' side. He tried to pass a law to get them a vote in the country but those damn democrats blocked it and I don't really know why.' But she was only half aware what he was saying at the time because she had her eyes on two men standing beside that rude lady and her big husband and she mentioned she thought they looked sinister to him and said, 'Those two are up to something bad I feel it strongly!' She persuaded a very reluctant William to confront them face to face with her right behind him and he did it cautiously. Sure enough each of them was concealing a pistol under his coat. Out came one of the guns, straight into William's face and that was a big mistake by the gunman because he grabbed the barrel so quick, he didn't have time to divert his weapon.

When Little Stick saw that she quickly confronted the other one and drew her skinning knife out from her belt and waved it in front of his face and then stuck it under his throat and told him with venom, 'Mister, give me the gun or I will slit you right down to your little pee wee. I am a full Cherokee and an expert skinner, this is not a request!' She then pierced his skin with the tip and gazed straight into his eyes and he dropped his pistol to the ground with sheer fear at the very thought of it but it was already fully cocked and it went off by that impact and the bullet hit William's leg. But William kept a firm grip of the other gun's barrel and when that happened all the crowd around them gave them a lot of space while four of the President's men ran over to them. The rude lady shouted to the first one on the scene, 'I saw it all. This man and his filthy Indian friend tried to shoot the President.' But William told them, 'Do not listen to

103

that mad old girl these two are the ones. We stopped them the minute they drew their pistols because she spotted them way before they began to make their move!' Of course they hauled in both of them as well just for a few questions.

They questioned Little Stick at first who was not happy at all and she went absolutely ballistic with all of these foolish questions they asked her and they put her in a completely separate room from him with a lady security guard. This lady had neither been on the scene or even out there and she only knew that a lady pointed Little Stick out and that the lady's husband was in congress so it must be dealt with in the proper manner. After another silly remark, Little Stick just went to town and stated, 'That mad old bat is just blind with ignorance and prejudice and full of untruths and just plain rude. She is obnoxious, offensive and a total liar, so there. Can I leave now and tend to my friend's leg? He has a bullet in it for saving your top man!' and the lady guard told her, 'You are free to leave,' and added, 'Don't forget your knife!' She handed it to her and off Little Stick went down that long corridor looking for someone to give her some information about William. There he was standing at the entrance on two feet without a grimace and he informed her, 'All done. They fixed me up. It is only a graze wound,' and asked her, 'So what about you?' and she replied smiling, 'I will survive. I have been through a lot worse than that,' and then she slipped her hand into his.

They headed to the hotel that Fred had recommended and it wasn't too posh looking but it seemed adequate for a one night stay so in they went towards the lady on reception and he asked for a room with twin beds and breakfast in the morning for just one night. 'Fine no problem' she replied, 'we can fit you in,' and added, 'Who is the young lady?' Rather foolishly he stated, 'Don't asked me ask her.' Little Stick was already fully wound up and she stated not too pleasantly, 'I have got a mouth and a brain and I am a fully qualified optometrist just like him I am not his possession I am a free woman and always will be!' The receptionist politely replied with an explanation and said, 'Sorry for asking, it is just my job to get full details of all the people in the hotel for security because it is so close to the White House!' 'I know' exclaimed Little Stick, 'we have just been there!' and then they popped into the lounge for a quick coffee to recover from today's events. Then in stepped two people from the White House and they asked the reception lady, 'We are looking for a couple, Mr Newlands and an Indian girl, are they staying here?' and she replied, 'They certainly are but don't ask her any funny questions because she will bite your head off!' The lady remarked, 'Don't worry we have met her before. Tell them they have been invited to dinner in the house with the President!' The receptionist replied, 'Tell them yourself, they are sitting in the coffee room right in the corner,' and when they walked in Little Stick exclaimed, 'Holy shit it is them again, we have told them everything!' and then she ducked under the table. The lady called out, 'Okay, nothing to worry about, they confessed everything under severe questioning and the

President would like to meet both of you over dinner at the White House. Are you free tonight?' William replied, 'It is our pleasure we will be there!' and the lady said, 'We will send a carriage to pick you up from here,' and told Little Stick, 'You can come out now!' She then reappeared and asked him, 'Did I hear right that we are to meet the President over dinner in the White House?' and he replied, 'Spot on, you clever girl.'

Their carriage arrived at precisely six thirty that evening. It was a really chilly night and she was very grateful of her new coat and hat and in they went to the most gorgeous home they had ever seen. Out came a team of people to lead the way to their destination and it was truly magnificent and her eyes could not adjust to so much splendour but she wasn't short of words and she asked many questions to the people who assisted them inside but she did not get one single reply. They entered the big dining room and straight away she noticed the table was only set for four places and she chatted happily with his good lady and confessed to her, 'I know nothing about politics!' and she replied, 'Me neither,' and they both had a little giggle. Then she asked Little Stick, 'Would you really have slit his throat, I mean of course the man with the gun?' and she gaily replied, 'Sure I would and he knew that because I looked him straight in the eyes and told him so. When I nicked him in the throat he dropped the pistol.' The first lady then asked her, 'So how long have you been in New York?' and she told her, 'About five years. I met him when he was travelling in the Great Plains with a wagon all the way from New York and he is my warrior with no fear whatsoever. I love him to bits and I persuaded my dad to let me go with him to the big city when I was nearly fourteen and he agreed. Isn't that something!' She then asked Mrs Grant, 'Would you like me to help you to clean up?' and she responded sweetly, 'No, no, that is not really necessary we have got people to do that but thanks for the offer.' William was on first names terms with the President by now, but not on politics, on working men's lives in both America and England.

Soon it was time for their departure and the President handed William a cheque for two thousand dollars, a small fortune to him, for his quick action and in came a man and said, 'Your carriage awaits you to take you back to your hotel.' On their way there she remarked, 'Such lovely normal people. I would vote for him any day,' and he stated, 'You cannot now. Maybe sometime in the near future. It may happen sooner than you think!' And up they treaded to their room.

The first comment she made, when she stepped into the room was, 'Why are there two beds?' and he replied, 'It cuts down the temptation for me but I don't know about you!' She cheekily remarked, 'Well I don't really know, I will just carry on as usual being myself,' and added, 'My dad isn't here. It has been five years since you made that vow and you won me in that contest remember!' He answered limply, 'I need a good sleep tonight after all that business today, please don't wake me,' and she replied, 'Oh you poor baby, would I do that!' Just after he turned down the oil lamp, she slid silently out of her bed and into his and said, 'Give me a big cuddle to make me sleep better,' and he did that out of sheer habit because he now found her totally irresistible. When she got that close to him and when he gazed into her eyes his power to resist her just melted away like water running down into a stream. But if he was in company or doing business for the shop or even in the public eye he could just switch off his feelings for her faster than a blink of an eye.

Right now he made no complaint about the intrusion in his personal space and he even turned over to face her and that pleased her immensely. Then she kissed him all over but never ventured anywhere near his wounded leg. Still she had no positive reaction from him because he still had his promise to her dad on his mind. She presumed that was all in the past but not for him because he was a man of his word. Then she realised that this wasn't going to be a night of passion but she still cuddled up close to him and then she went back into her own bed and had sweet dreams of him in her sleep. At seven the next morning both were wide awake and went down to a hearty breakfast and then caught their train back to New York. His leg was almost back to normal and she danced all the way to the station. There they met that rude lady and her husband yet again and they walked straight past her. But then Little Stick stopped and turned around and announced loudly, 'We had dinner in the White House with the President last night,' gleefully and added, 'No thanks to you, you blind old bat!' and that made her feel a lot better.

William then remarked, 'Now that was not very nice,' and she retorted, 'Well she isn't very nice!' and then she skipped onto the train making sure they got into a separate carriage and said to him, 'Thanks for that really exciting day!' and then she kissed him on the cheek and he replied, 'It was nothing to do with me you did it all by yourself.' She smiled at that and remarked, 'Maybe so, but not without my new warrior. You were quick to react in the face of danger and stood there face to face with a killer and removed his gun quick as a flash. Only then did I confront the other one with my skinning knife and made him drop his pistol which then shot you, so sorry about that!' and then she gave a little giggle.

They arrived in New York without any further incidents and he decided to walk the route home because he reckoned that was good for his leg. This time she actually walked alongside him just in case he suddenly toppled over but he didn't and he made it all the way there under his own steam while gritting his teeth a few times. She opened the door for him and Nicole remarked as they entered, 'The mystery couple has landed!' and asked Roseanne to call the boys down and tell them they are back in one piece and then said to William, 'It was all in the morning papers and we guessed it must be you two. Am I right?' 'Spot on' he replied, 'Little Miss Hawkeye spotted them from quite a distance and said we must stop them – "you take the big one and I will take the little fellow" and that is it.' Nicole then stated, 'There were no names mentioned, was that your request?' and he replied, 'Absolutely, I don't want my name splashed all of the papers. I like my nice quiet life just as it is.' Then he revealed to her, 'We had dinner last night with the President and his wife in the White House, no less. He is a really fine chap and she got on pretty well with the wife,' and added, 'I am so glad we are back in one piece!'

Now he had to work every night to complete the order from Quebec and she wasn't that pleased but he did manage a few short lessons on her chosen instrument at that time because he knew in two weeks' time she was going to perform with the band nightly. He made a decision to tell Fred about her latest venture and he took it rather well he thought but then he gave him a lecture about drug taking and spiked drinks and other mishaps on the road to fame in the music business and told him to pass it on to Little Stick. He did just that but she pooh-poohed that path and said, 'I would never do such a thing. I have a brain in my head and it works pretty well!' and he accepted that, and left it there.

Then he thought "gosh what will her dad think about this new career? Will he hit the roof and blame it on me? Now that wouldn't go down well with my reputation for looking after her well whilst she's in the big city". But he realised that she was no longer a little girl lost in New York and was perfectly capable of looking after herself in any situation. So he told her 'this Sunday we will go down to the pub because now you are nearly ready to perform with the guitar and sing along with it' and she remarked, 'Really great, I like that little bar a lot it is quite relaxing and it gives me a good buzz to sing there.' Sure enough when they stepped in there the fiddle player spotted her just after the band had tuned up and waved her over and said to her, 'Well are you ready to sing tonight?!' Just then he spotted her guitar and remarked, 'I never knew you could play as well?' and she replied, 'Only thanks to him. He rushed me through some lessons in the past few weeks!' and added, 'Just let me catch my breath, I will join you in the second half.' She and William took a seat at the nearby table next to the stage and he got their drinks and they settled down to watch their performance.

The venue quickly filled up with lots of people and when they saw her going up on the stage they gave her a massive cheer and she responded with a grin of delight and a little strum of her guitar. Then she sang her heart out with a rousing first song and then broke into a little medley of country songs and the band just slipped in behind the rhythm of her beating the guitar with that slapping technique that he had taught her. William had thought "well, she has obviously been practising for this little event but is it just for fun or maybe a brand new career in the music business? She really likes the attention and she has a good set of lungs to do the job, that little band needs an extra spark and she has definitely got it if this takes off big time. I will be in real trouble with Fred because he doesn't like anyone to mess him around but then again she is a vital member of the team in the shop and also on the road. Maybe he could come to some sort of compromise with her so that she could do both of them. But where does that leave me? Would I have to go with her every night? – no that would be almost impossible".

Then back she came to their table and the band finished their set without her. After that little show he seriously thought he just may be able to convince Fred that it was vital to keep her on as a part time assistant as she was about to take her career into a completely unusual vocation. He walked her home silently but thoughtful, while she was chatting away about her performance and the crowd reaction. But he uttered not a word because next week she would go full time with the band and that didn't sit nicely with him and on Monday morning he would have a serious talk with Fred about her position in the shop and her right to stay there. Now Fred wasn't a monster at all but he did have strict rules about staff and about the way he ran the business but also was very open about suggestions in ways that he could compromise. William felt he could put forward a few ideas that would fit into his way of thinking but it must seem quite plausible to him and fit into the shop's needs.

William decided to approach him on the matter that following day at lunchtime because after he had eaten he was in a much better mood. He had already formulated a plan of suitability for her working hours in the shop and he put it to Fred. Fred responded, 'That will solve the problem for me because she will need all the beauty sleep after performing all those nights in smoky venues up to nearly midnight but tell her I need a little chat with her before she starts on that rocky road,' and William replied, 'Will do.'

Chapter Twelve

Little Stick now had only one week before she hit the road full time and she was both excited and concerned. And now panic set in along with other thoughts but she knew that her warrior was always close at hand and that thought gave her the courage to carry on looking at the bright side of life. Even though he wasn't with her exactly he was always close by and willing to help her in her push for a better life and always ready to give her a much-needed cuddle and that was enough for her for now because without him she would be still living on the reservation back in Oklahoma bored to tears and still dreaming about the big outside world. With all these new things happening day by day he was still not the perfect man she thought he could be but she wouldn't change him for anybody else.

This little band were playing five nights a week now but that would increase in time to seven. That presented him with a problem because he knew he could not give up his work in the shop that long and he thought he might just lose her to someone else. But when he put this question to her at the wrong moment, she snapped back, 'You silly boy that would never happen to us!' But he wasn't convinced at the time because he knew she was quite fond of many cuddles. So was he also after he met her but there is always that thought in his mind. Anyway, the week before her going full time with the band he took it upon himself to teach her a few more little riffs on the guitar so that she was fully prepared for the project. She had indicated that she was rather nervous to take it on but with his gentle art of saying the right words, she was now looking forward to the challenge of performing in front of a mainly white man's audience. Okay, she had done it before but that was in a local venue in which all of the people seemed rather friendly. This next step was way beyond that and she did feel rather apprehensive about performing at venues she had never been to. But his quiet reassurances made her feel much more self-confident and she started off her new career in a place named Buffalo not too far away from New York and he went with her to give some moral support. But that was not needed because, once she was on stage, all the fears simply disappeared and she performed like she had done before and that brought a grin to his face while he sat quietly at his table. After it was all over and she came over to the table and asked him, 'What do you think?' he simply replied, 'What do you think!' and she stated, 'I feel tingly all over' He remarked, 'You should do. You knocked them over. They loved you, but don't let it go to your head for now!'

She was playing with this little band four or five evenings a week and around New York City and some places just outside the city limits. That was no big problem for him because he could manage to get there and back home at a reasonable time for both of them either by train or the band's own personal wagon which was only used for close at hand venues. One of them was called Stamford and it was quite a large venue and now and again a bit rowdy but that didn't really affect the band's performance on stage because they were all used to it. Little Stick wasn't and she had to raise her voice a lot more than usual but it was well within her capabilities to finish the song in tune and in time.

One big ruckus was going on just at her left quite near the front where she was singing and where William was sitting and he saw the whole incident erupting quite clearly with some man slapping a young lady sitting next to him and then with a clenched fist preparing to punch her. He did and William knew he just had to intervene. So he stood up facing the man and told him to behave himself in his usual quiet manner but this man took a swing at him. Fortunately he saw it coming, blocked it with his left arm and then punched him with his right fist and sent him flying onto the next table into another chap who was sitting there. The man wasn't very happy with this and he challenged William to step outside. He did just that quickly followed by the nice young lady who was most apologetic for the trouble she had caused him. But he brushed her aside and said, 'No worries, I can handle him,' and then he addressed the man who was standing there with fists raised and told him quietly, 'I didn't intend to hit him that hard, it was just a natural reaction on my part!' Hearing this the man held out one of his hands and said to him, 'No big problem you are a true gentleman. He was really getting on my nerves with all that shouting and cursing at her. No need for all that, I think he has a slate loose in his head.' Then two of the doormen threw the rowdy one out into the street just where they were standing.

Then that nice young lady stepped outside to make sure her hero was okay and to thank him once more and then she asked him, 'Can I sit with you for the rest of the evening?' and he then put his arm around her in a protective way and said, 'It is my pleasure. My, you have a pretty face apart from that big bruise on your jaw.' Then she introduced herself saying, 'My name is Ramona,' and added with a smile, 'You have done that before I can tell, with your quiet assurance and freedom from doubt that you will ever lose, am I right?' William replied, 'Please, no more, you will get me blushing, Ramona,' and she added, 'And modest as well. I like that in a man.' He stated flatly, 'I just came here to listen to the band.' She had no intention of losing this new man that just walked into her life and she kept dead quiet until the band's interval. Then Little Stick came over to their table. He had already got a drink in for her and in between sips, she remarked, 'That was quite a rowdy session I could hardly hear myself sometimes,' and only then, she glanced at the lady sitting next to him and remarked to her, 'Now that is quite a nasty bruise you have there,' and added, 'Were you in that fight?' She sweetly replied, 'No not me. This handsome man saved me with one well aimed hit!' and Little Stick responded, 'I bet he did!' and then she added, 'And you are?' William broke in just there and said to Ramona, 'Meet Little Stick, the most beautiful Cherokee lady born in my lifetime!' and

116

then added foolishly, 'We are not really a couple but we do look out for each other.' Then Ramona extended her hand and said with a great smile, 'I am Ramona, pleased to meet you,' and added, 'You are a good singer. I have heard many but you are one of the best and I also like your neat little band, tight as a drum in my ears!' Little stick dropped her fixed glare and smiled sweetly to this pretty lady and replied, 'Thank you for that,' and went back up to join her band in the dressing room.

At the end of the night after a blazing second half with a few encores and light beer, Little Stick was back in top form with her confidence fully regained but the last thing she expected was to see pretty Ramona still sitting with him at their table. Over she came and she was not very pleased with this sight and he pre-read her mindset because he could see that fire in her eyes. So he explained the situation to her and asked her, could she persuade the driver of the wagon to drop her off at her apartment and added, 'Because her boyfriend just might be waiting outside to do her some more damage!' Little Stick retorted laconically, 'Oh really, so just how far away is your block?' and Ramona answered, 'About five streets away going north, and if that is a problem with you I am just going to chance it!' Little Stick replied, 'Well we are all going south to the city . . .'

William then intervened and said, 'Just ask Gary himself. After all it is his wagon. I am sure he wouldn't mind being out of his way for just a few minutes?' and she answered flatly, 'No way, we are all very tired, we want to head home as quickly as possible,' and he retorted, 'Okay be like that I will walk her home myself and catch a later train back!' Ramona interjected and said, 'I don't want to cause any trouble between you two. I will go by myself. My apologies to both of you, if I do get beaten up again no sweat, I can take it!' He decided there and then that he would take her home and said to her, 'Okay let us go right now, no more chat!' and off they went down the darkened streets and she silently slipped her arm through his and said to herself, "Now I feel very safe".

William didn't even notice, until the man jumped out from the dark at him, and he then unattached her arm and threw a punch at him straight on the nose. He dropped to the sidewalk and didn't move and just lay there like a sleeping cat and he commented to Ramona, 'Now some people just cannot learn.' She then revealed, 'My block is just around the corner,' and asked him to come in for a coffee and of course he did but mentioned, 'Just a quick one I have a train to catch,' and she then smiled from ear to ear after she unlocked the main door.

She then asked him, 'Are you some sort of a fighter?' and he shyly replied, 'No not at all it is just a few little defence moves I have picked up on the streets of London.' She remarked, 'So that is where the strange accent comes from, so you are English yes?' and he replied, 'Yes I am certainly from London, England. We came over here a few years ago to set up an opticians – that is me and my two colleagues – and we are doing rather well. It is a shop called Scarlets in the middle of the town,' and Ramona stated, 'I know it well. I work for Optical Glass and we supply you with the sheets. I work in the sales department. Now isn't that strange, we are almost colleagues as well!' After he had finished his third cup of coffee he got rather anxious and stated, 'I must go now to catch my train home,' and she then suggested, 'You can stay here tonight. I have got a lovely big couch you can sleep on and catch the early train in the morning. It is so much safer than travelling in the night!' He shyly rejected this offer and stated, 'I am a big boy and can handle any trouble I might meet.' She then explained to him, 'I do know that but you might just as well sleep over because all the thugs are out and about at this time of the night around here. Better be safe than sorry.' 'Well if that is the case,' he remarked sheepishly, 'okay, if it isn't any trouble for you I will.'

Then Ramona gave him a big smile and replied, 'Good boy, you know it makes sense,' and so he settled down for the night at her place and thoughtfully tended her bruised jaw with cold towels and some gentle massage and that made her feel a whole lot better. She was over the moon that he was staying the night there, even though he insisted that the couch was fine for him and while lying in her bed alone without that painful jaw she mused, "now sometime you have to give a little room to someone". She wasn't no manhunter but she did like a little tender care from a decent chap and she had actually got one in her room now and she mused once more and thought, "can I actually hang on to this one?". Then her thoughts turned to that fiery little Indian girl and reckoned maybe not, but she slept well that night.

The next morning she was up at the crack of dawn

and made him some pancakes and coffee before he left and while he was eating she wrote out her name and address on paper and slipped it inside his jacket pocket just on an off chance. He kissed her goodbye at the door, very lightly of course.

Meanwhile that same night the wagon dropped Little Stick off at the shop doorway but she had one big problem. That was that William had the key of the main door, not her. She searched the street for some little pebbles to chuck at Nicole's window but there were none around, so then she searched her pockets and found a few small coins and used them instead. Luckily she was an excellent thrower because although they were on the third floor all four coins hit the window and out popped Nicole's head and she called down, 'Now what is wrong?' When she saw there was no William she threw on a coat and rushed downstairs and opened the door to find a weeping Little Stick shivering in the cold night air. Then she picked up Little Stick's guitar and bag and hurried her upstairs into her room and asked her straight out, 'He is not dead is he?' and she revealed, 'No nothing as drastic as that. He is taking some pretty girl home to her apartment after a fight in the bar – you know what he is like!' After a little pause Nicole asked, 'So what was the problem in that. Surely you went with him to see her all right?' Little Stick remarked, 'No way, she is much too pretty,' and Nicole then answered, 'Now that is exactly why you should have gone with him, because pretty girls have a real problem catching good men. They usually end up with real bozos and you actually let her have him, you are a real silly girl. Sorry, it doesn't really work like that, big mistake on your part and wipe your silly face dry!' and then she added, 'Don't let him out of sight for a moment because he is not your average guy. He has never had a girl in his life before and so he doesn't know how to handle them and some lucky lady just might snatch him away from you given half a chance. So tread very carefully in the future and don't take him for granted.' Little Stick took all of this information about men into her smart little head and she was really furious with herself about not letting Ramona ride in the wagon for a few streets because she knew full well that he was very strong minded.

She didn't hear that big door open even though she listened intensely for those heavy boots walking up the stairs – but to no avail and it was just gone three in the morning, not a sound, when she crawled into her own bed with regrets. William got back to the shop at six thirty and went straight into his apartment for a quick wash and shave, then he cut through the little connecting tunnel and straight into the workshop and donned his leather apron ready for a day's work. Neither of his two male colleagues had any idea that he had stayed out all night and of course he said nothing. But now Little Stick was in a panic that she hadn't seen him and she had no idea that he was upstairs because she rarely had any reason to go up there.

At lunchtime he stepped down the stairs lightly and said cheerfully, 'Good afternoon, ladies, nice sunny day outside but a bit nippy also.' Nicole asked him quizzically straight out, 'So where were you all night?' and added, 'We sat up all night for you.' He responded, 'No need for that I can look after myself!' with a straight face and then explained to her, 'I stayed overnight with a distressed young lady in her apartment and I soothed her bruised jaw and the boyfriend was waiting for her outside to give her some more. So to me that is a job well done because I disposed of him as well.' A furious Little Stick retorted, 'I bet you did a good job on him,' and he replied, 'Tut tut, no need to lose your hair. You should have come with me. She is a real nice lady and she made me breakfast in the morning!' That remark hit a raw spot in her mind so Nicole put her arm around her and said, 'There there, calm yourself down. That hot little temper will get you in big trouble sooner rather than later. Just let him explain and listen. Don't just make up your mind before you hear the whole truth.' William then remarked, 'No need to explain further. The lady was in trouble and I offered to see her home safely and the man was waiting outside of her block with a knife ready to cut her up. So I knocked him flat and I would do it again. It is just my way and I don't need anyone to run my life. I don't run anyone else's life so why should I let someone run mine?' Little Stick then realised that this man would go his own way just like her and this revelation made her even more proud of him but now she realised she must be a bit more careful of her actions towards him.

They all headed down to their little cafe for a spot of lunch and who was sitting in there? It was only pretty Ramona, who never dreamed she would meet him again so soon. She gave him a big smile when he entered the doorway. Little Stick froze on the spot but after that slight hesitation a thought flashed through her mind and she realised that this was a pure fluke, no one could plan this far ahead not even this pretty lady. She knew that William would never do that and if he did, he wouldn't invite everyone along with him. So she returned the smile and remarked lightly, 'Fancy seeing you in here,' and added, 'So how is your jaw now?' and she replied, 'At least I can eat again properly.' Now Nicole was really curious and she asked this young lady, 'Are you Ramona?' and she replied, 'I am she, and you are?' and she replied, 'Nicole! We all work in Scarlet's.' She extended her hand to shake and she did just that and William then remarked, 'Your face is almost back to normal you look real good,' and then he kissed her on the forehead gently.

Little Stick shifted very uncomfortably in her seat when she saw that and Nicole gently took her hand and said to her, 'Don't worry it is just his nature, there is nothing in it.' Little Stick retorted, 'It is my man. He cannot kiss someone in a public place like that. She is so damn pretty!' But Nicole remarked, 'Why have you got green eyes for this? I would never believe it from someone so independent like you, denying your man from kissing some pretty girl. You really have to get a grip on yourself!' Then Ramona stated, 'I was down this way to look for another apartment because I reported the attack to the police and they advised me to move out and find another place to live because he might just try it again. But I didn't tell them the whole truth and I told them a passing stranger held him back so I could enter my block safely. I didn't mention you stayed with me overnight.' Now Nicole had a firm grip of both of Little Stick's wrists when he said to Ramona, 'Ah you poor little thing,' and then he kissed her cheek softly.

Then she revealed, 'My boss gave me the day off to find another place, isn't that sweet of him and now I have a free day but I don't really know this area.' Now after the girls heard the whole story Nicole let loose her grip on Little Stick and she told Ramona, 'There is a nice block not too far away from here at a fairly reasonable rate with no riff raff present that would probably suit you well if you like. I will take you there now. I have got a few minutes left before I have to go back.' 'Fine by me,' she replied and off they went to view it.

William then remarked to Little Stick, 'Such a pleasant young lady,' and she simply grunted back, 'If you like that sort, I suppose!' Now he never knew she was the jealous type and took no notice at the time and just replied, 'Fine.'

Ramona simply loved this new apartment in the block that Nicole had taken her to because it was neat and secure with an iron gate in front of the main door. She had a chat to the live-in landlord and he told her she could move in tonight so then she asked Nicole, 'Can you help me to get it sorted tonight? I have quite a lot of stuff. I am a sort of artist.' 'Sure' Nicole answered, 'I am free tonight. No trouble to me, it is kind of nice to have a new face around. I will meet you here at six thirty, okay!' to which she replied, 'Great see you then.' Off went Nicole back to the shop and she told the other two, 'She took it and she will move in tonight,' and added, 'I am going to help her move her bits in.' William said, 'Maybe we will go with you and then we will all go out for something to eat. It would make a nice change to being stuck indoors,' and Little Stick also grunted her approval and said, 'Fine by me.' Then she asked Nicole, 'You really like her?' and she responded, 'She is a sweet girl and very well spoken too.' But Little Stick was still harbouring that jealous streak and stated back with a grimace, 'She is too damn pretty, she just might be trouble!' But Nicole stuck to her guns and said, 'You are talking poo.'

William had gone upstairs back into his workshop by then and he had still no idea that she thought Ramona was competition to her. But while they were walking to Ramona's new block it all spilled out and she stated frankly, 'Look she is just a total stranger to us, why help her out!' This remark really annoyed him and he retorted, 'Look, we were strangers once, just what is your problem? We are helping her out because she is in big trouble. We need to make sure she is safe and that is just good people helping other good people and that is what makes the world go round!' Then she remarked, 'You just don't understand do you?' and he replied, 'No I really don't. I took the sensible course to stay there overnight because the streets around there were full of thugs at night so I played it safe and I caught the first train back in the morning.' 'But what about me?' she asked, 'You had the key. I couldn't get in,' and he remarked, 'You are a real clever girl. I knew you could find a way in and anyway I asked you to come with me remember?' At this, down went her head and she replied, 'She is much too pretty,' and he remarked with a smile, 'A much better reason to come with me, you silly girl.' So now it was revealed, all out in the open. She had dropped that steely stoic independent attitude and that brought an even bigger smile to his face and he kissed her gently on each cheek. Then they caught up with Nicole who was sensibly well ahead of them and a wagon rolled up right in front of the block with Ramona waving at them.

There were two men with her in the wagon to help her unload her bits and pieces and to lift out the heavy items and they did it with the help of her three new volunteers. Now it was all in behind that steel gate in front of the main door. About an hour later, just when they were lifting smaller items upstairs, along came three rough looking men and one of them was her ex-boyfriend. William spotted him from a distance and told the girls, 'Now here comes trouble!' and Ramona questioned, 'So how does he know I was moving here?' William answered, 'You must have told someone, maybe a friend or someone in your office' and she revealed, 'I had mentioned it to my flatmate but she is a bit thick and she doesn't really like me at all.' 'Now that is where he got it from,' he remarked and added, 'So let's all face them head on. I will take the big one and you three take the other two. All right, let's go!' Out they came with Little Stick screaming battle cries with her skinning knife held high just in case someone may be armed and the ex-boyfriend was her chosen target. He did have a knife but he was no match for this little screaming Cherokee and he dropped it in sheer terror. She took him down in seconds and sat on him and said, 'Mister, I am going to skin you alive head to belly!' and she placed the tip of her knife into his throat and said to him in a quiet voice, 'Just leave my friend alone in future otherwise I will truly slit your throat right now!' Nicole and Ramona took care of the third man fairly quickly, then grinned at each other and slapped each other's hands for doing a good job on him and Ramona then locked the gate. They went off for a bite to eat in a sweet little bar not too far away whilst the three men rose from the sidewalk and left the scene in a poor state rather sheepishly for their failure to overcome three young ladies, because they thought they were all tough guys.

They went back into the apartment after that little tumble for a quick wash and brush up before they went out to eat and Little Stick remarked, 'Now that was a bundle of fun, it is a long time since I had one of them.' Nicole then remarked to Ramona, 'You are quite a little fighter. I thought all pretty girls were a bit soft and sweet but you did all right on the night,' and she revealed, 'Under pressure we are fearsome if we have the back up.' William then said, 'Okay ladies time to move on let's find somewhere to replenish ourselves.' Ramona replied, 'This meal is on me for my new found friends. Thank you all for your help and saving my sanity as well as my life!' She picked a cosy little Italian place and they all ordered spaghetti with meatballs because it was fun to eat after a hard night's tussle, along with a few bottles of wine and in there they all bonded as one.

Just after he went to the gent's room, Ramona said, 'What a lovely evening. Thanks to both of you and of course to sweet William. You have got a real gem there.' As always Little Stick was still searching for information on him and she asked her flatly, 'So did you sleep with him when he stayed at your place overnight?' But she pooh-poohed that enquiry and replied, 'No chance. He slept on my couch – his decision not mine.' Then Little Stick asked her, 'Would you sleep with him if he asked you?' and her reply was a definite one word answer; and that was, 'AbsoBLOODYlutely!' Now that response she didn't expect from such a pretty lady but she did respect her honest answer and she then thought to herself "maybe I was a little hard on her at first". But then again she must look after herself whatever the cost. Now they were friends at heart after that little tussle but she knew she had to keep a close eye on her for now. William arrived back on the scene none the wiser about that conversation.

During the following week, after lunchtime, in popped the fiddle player from her band and he pleaded with her to do a slot in Toronto saying, 'I know you don't want to travel too far but this gig would be very good for the band. It is this coming Saturday and we would love you to be there. It is one big venue and quite a lot of the people in the business will be there – please will you come?' After a little thought she replied, 'Okay, I will be there. I will meet you in the station at the usual place bang on time.' William then interjected and said to her, 'Sorry, I can't make it because there is a rather big order in the workshop that has to be ready on Monday, but if we finish early I will be there later on.'

Chapter Thirteen

So that was all settled in the meantime and, come the said evening, all went to plan. Nicole also stayed behind to pack the goods in boxes and in her lunchtime she dropped into Ramona's place and asked her for some help with the packing. Ramona agreed straight away and answered, 'Sure no problem, I have nothing on tonight, so at least it gets me out on a Saturday night.' The three men also did their bit, packing along with the two girls and then it was all sorted and finished. William then stated, 'I am now off to Toronto to catch the end of her performance, it is always the best bit!' and then he asked the two girls, 'Do you want to come too?' Nicole replied, 'Yes I will come. I have never been to Canada.' Then in chimed Ramona with a 'Me too.' So after a quick brush up and wash they all headed to the station for that not-too-long journey into Canada.

When they got there, William bagged a carriage to take them to the principal hall and the driver said, 'I know where it is, it is a big night tonight I believe!' and William remarked back, 'I guess so.' In they went and sat at the table nearest the stage. It wasn't too loud for them being that close and Little Stick was in full swing when they came in. The band were into their last set, so no one noticed their arrival and both girls went straight to the bar for some drinks and a few free snacks. Then Little Stick spotted him sitting at the table and thought "good, he made it". Then the band wrapped up their performance after three encores. The people were still shouting for more but they went backstage eventually to have some talks with music promoters and a quick light beer and after that Little Stick headed straight to the table where William sat. She gave a quick glance over his head and saw Ramona with a tray full of drinks heading straight for the table and she stated accusingly, 'IT'S YOU?' and then right behind her, Nicole called out, 'AND ME!' Now that little scene threw Little Stick quite off balance and Nicole took her to one side and told her straight, 'Look young lady, you really need to get a grip on yourself, she is a nice young girl she has no intention of taking your man away from you. She helped me out by packing away the goods so that he could make it here on time, so just calm down and make friends with her. We both just wanted to be here to see you perform on the big day.' 'I am so sorry, will do,' replied Little Stick and back they went to their table.

He still had no idea about the way girls think but he was more than pleased to see her smile again and then she broke into a song quite out of the blue and Ramona remarked, 'I quite like this one,' and she sung it with her, in perfect harmony. This was overheard by the fiddle player and the lady guitarist and they both came over and joined in and he said to Ramona, 'Now my band could use someone like you, after Little Stick has left!' Ramona responded with a hesitant, 'Maybe, if she doesn't mind,' while nodding to her fellow singer and Little Stick remarked, 'No skin off my nose. You are all right, you sing pretty well. Let us sing together in our local pub next Sunday. It is a sweet little place with a good crowd!' Ramona said, a little nervously, 'Will do, but I am a touch rusty on some songs,' to which Little Stick remarked, 'No problem. Just follow me like you did then.' Then the guitarist enquired, 'So what is your name?' and she proudly announced her name, saying, 'I am Ramona Cattona from sunny Mexico. I came here looking for work when I was sixteen and I eventually found it after many bad choices and that made me pretty tough but now and again you make another choice and I suppose that is life itself!' Then Little Stick gave her a big hug and said, 'Welcome to my land. No more hard feelings from me you are alright!' William had never seen someone change their attitude that fast in his whole life and he just stared in amazement at the two pretty girls hugging in front of him and then Nicole gave a quick round of applause, the rest of them joined in and the two of them re-started that song they were singing along with the two band members.

So it was all quiet on the western front at the moment, "but will it last?" he thought to himself. Of course, he had no idea about girls but slowly and surely he would pick it up in time because right now he was only interested in making his life better than before, which was why he had jumped at the chance to go to America with the other two. They picked up Ramona that following Sunday evening as all three of them walked to the pub and, yes, Nicole was there too because she would not miss this event when they would sing together in front of a live audience. She thought "so how will it turn out?" and she asked him the same question and he remarked confidently, 'Let us just find out. I am pretty sure they will be all right together,' as the two of them were up in front chatting away just like old friends. When she saw that, Nicole remarked to him, 'I just couldn't imagine that could happen so suddenly last night. One minute she was spitting fire at her and now she is as sweet as a sixpence,' and he remarked, 'It must be an old Indian trick!' with a grin. Then he remarked, 'I believe that her brain is full of little buttons, both hot and cold and I reckon that she has no control over them but that her mood swings are in complete control. Now, I am no doctor but I'm completely sure that is the answer. I don't understand girls at all – they are far too complicated for me – but I still like them. You are not like that at all, you fit in with the boys pretty easily!' and she retorted with a little grin, 'Don't you believe that, I only do that out of sheer survival in a man's world. Because if women got a vote in your world things would be a lot better for us. Just watch this space!' He remarked, 'I never knew that women were into politics,' and Nicole replied, 'Men never give it a thought because they think we are only possessions, but of course I am not referring to you.' 'I hope not,' he said, and then they all trooped into the pub which was almost packed out already and they only just managed to grab a table.

Then the fiddle player called the two girls over and announced to the audience, 'And tonight on stage we will have three pretty girls to sing to you. Meet the newie, she is called Ramona and she has quite a voice just like Little Stick so tonight you will hear something extra special. So fill up your jugs and tune in your ears, we will be on stage at the usual time. Just give us some time to tune up!' William remarked to Nicole, 'He is quite professional to warm up the people before they even begin.' Then they started playing, with Little Stick slapping her strings with a drumstick driving the melody along and then both girls came in with their harmonies, just as though they had been doing it for years. Their opening number was a real belter just as they planned and it went down really well with this crowd. So it was a total success due to Ramona, who held back her fear in front of such an audience after a little practice backstage for both of them with the guitarist.

After the first session they both went back to their table and Nicole remarked, 'You sound super together and I was totally impressed,' and William agreed with that comment and said, 'I got you both a light beer just to loosen you up before you go on again.' Ramona picked up the jug and said, 'Cheers,' and then stated, 'I was a bit nervous up there but she pulled me through it with her little glances just to put me on the right track and after a few minutes I was into the flow,' 'No one noticed that,' he remarked, 'you did all right but now you both have to choose, is the life for you touring up and down the country or just doing local venues around here because that is the choice you have to make. I believe this little band will go somewhere beyond that!' After that little lecture both girls stared at each other silently and paused at the thought of it. Then he said, 'It is your life. You only have one crack at it. You make a great team up there!' Little Stick finally responded, 'We will do it full time together and hang the consequences if there are any!' Then they went back to the band to prepare for their second set and that was even better than the first. Afterwards they revealed to the band, 'We will do it together full time on the road!' and the fiddle player remarked, 'That will be magic, thank you girls.' Meanwhile back at their table he and Nicole were working out the severity of the consequences and how to reveal it to Fred who ran a very tight ship and did not like any messing around.

The short walk home was full of chatter about their future with two distinct views in opposite directions but they did it quietly without any raised voices and Little Stick suggested to Ramona, 'Stay over with me tonight so that we can discuss it further!' and she agreed. So they all went straight into the big room and William then stated abruptly with a solemn face, 'If you do this full time you do know you would have to give up your apartment because really you will have left the firm?' At this Little Stick's face went completely blank because that had never crossed her mind and she thought she was always part of the team. But she hadn't balanced this out in her head. She carefully thought about it and then suggested, 'Maybe I could just rent it from the firm!' and his reply was short but not so sweet as he said, 'It is not up to me, you will have to discuss it with Fred.'

That gave her something more to think about and

she mulled that in her head and asked herself, "So just how much money can I make out in this band, surely enough to cover my rent?" The very same question had crossed Ramona's mind as she gazed around this well-furnished room and she thought "this must cost her a small fortune". She asked Little Stick straight out, 'How much does this place cost you now?' and she replied, 'It comes free with the job and that is why I don't want to lose it. Just wait until you see my private apartment upstairs. And his apartment is downstairs, he is my true warrior, he even planned the whole set up in here.' Ramona exclaimed, 'What a truly amazing young man in these times. No wonder you gave me a hard time at first' and after their little get together was over they all headed to their separate abodes. When Ramona entered Little Stick's apartment, she thought it was even better than she imagined and said, 'I just love that big couch,' and Little Stick responded, 'Good, you are sleeping on it!'

In the workshop, William told Fred, 'She is staying in the band full time but wants to keep her apartment,' and he grimaced slightly at that remark and replied, 'She can but it will cost her!' William replied, 'Don't worry about the cost I will pay for it.' But Fred shook his head and said, 'No way, she should pay. She is no longer a young girl, she is now a grown woman and she will have to face the consequences of her actions and sort it out for herself!' And he added, 'Find yourself a nice little quiet lassie. Just have a look around there are plenty of them about.' But William had no intention of letting her go that easily, so he threw himself into his work most of the time that she was away and stayed in most evenings playing his guitar or reading some books. She and Ramona finally sorted out their living arrangements, because Ramona gave up her apartment and moved in to hers just to cover the cost of the rent that she had agreed with Fred.

Chapter Fourteen

꙳

From now on the band dropped all their smaller venues and went on the bigger ones, which of course were better paid, and they were on the road quite a lot more up and down the country. So really there was no time for a break to go back home and William missed all those little cuddles and that sweet smell of hers. She had been away almost eight months and William was feeling the lack of a pretty young girl and all those sweet little moments.

Now both of his colleagues upstairs in the workshop had observed this and Tim remarked to him, 'You are not fully at your best now are you?' and he replied, 'No not really, I just miss the company after hours in the evening.' Tim then suggested, 'Now what you need is a lady of the night that will do you good!' and then added, 'I know just the place. I use it four times a week. It makes me happy doing my job and if you want to try it come with me on Friday evening and bring along a good handful of silver dollars.' William of course had never been to such a place but he agreed to go with him just this once.

Now this place was down one of the darkest streets in the city he had ever been and it was a grubby little entrance through the front door. After a good pat down from the doorman they went in and he had never seen so many ladies in a state of undress and there were a whole line of them but a few of them were clothed. Tim told him, 'Just pick one, they are all willing,' and he then took a quick gulp of breath, paused in his choice and then picked out a little brown girl, fully dressed. She asked him, 'Why pick me? I am new to this,' and he retorted, 'Why not? You are a pretty girl!' and added, 'Me too, it is my first time in a place like this I just want a little chat and a cuddle that is all!' She stated firmly, 'It will cost you the same in advance, that is two dollars, one for me and one for the lady in charge.' He replied with a smile, 'No problem, I have brought many with me just in case I find a real treasure!' and now she was well intrigued.

She then had a long think about it and realised that this young man was quite serious but nevertheless she must do the procedure and she asked, 'So what do you want, shall I undress, or just lay on my back while you do it?' But he said, 'No, no, nothing like that, just a little cuddle and a chat,' and then he added, 'You are an Indian, so what tribe are you from?' She was getting really worried about him now and she answered reluctantly, 'I am Seminole from the Great Plains, I came down here to earn some dollars for my family and this is the only job I can find without the paperwork you need to get employment!' He stroked her pretty face and long dark hair and told her, 'I would give you an extra two dollars to help you out, but please no funny stuff with me!' and then she asked him, 'Why not? It is rather nice with the right person.' But then he rose from her bed and told her flatly, 'My best quality is to resist temptation!' and then he kissed her on the forehead and that made her smile.

He then put on his jacket and slipped into his boots and asked her directly, 'Can you clean rooms? If so I can get you a job in my shop. It is far safer than in here and it would probably pay you more. Think about it?' Quick as a flash, she replied, 'I will take it, thanks, boss!' Now he would have to explain her to Fred, who wasn't a hard man in some situations and who was always looking for someone to clean the shop. It was currently the girls' task and he was quite fussy about dusty desks and other furniture but he had a vital rule and that was that the cleaner must have a good reputation. Knowing this, William sat a while longer with this young girl and he related to her a little cover story about how he had met her and her previous position. She took all this in word for word and then he gave her the address of the shop and told her, 'Be there prompt at one o'clock and ask for William or Fred. Bring all your things too because we have a little spare room right at the top – it will suit you well!' and she replied, 'Will do,' and then he gave her a gentle peck on her nose and left.

When she appeared in the shop the next day with her little bundle, she asked Nicole, 'Would you like me to see either William or Fred about the cleaning job?' Of course Nicole knew nothing about it and so she called them down and informed them, 'A girl here about cleaning the shop.' They both came down together and William remarked, 'So you found it?' and she gave him a smile and Fred then put her to work straight away for a quick trial and she whizzed through the dusty pieces in the shop like a true professional. When she had finished, Fred told her, 'You can start tomorrow,' and only then he asked for her name and she replied, 'Jasmine,' with a big smile, and he remarked, 'Now that is quite a cute little name I think I could handle that rather well.' But this little cutie wouldn't be put off that easily and she volunteered to clean the whole shop right now for free and she told him, 'I don't have a place to sleep now because the old lady that employed me has passed way and her big house is now up for sale!' To this he replied, 'That is no big problem. We have a small room just at the top not in use. You can have that as part of the job with no charge.' Then he asked her to go to the cafe and gave her some money and told her, 'I want a bacon butty please.' She then whizzed out of the shop and into the cafe and in there were both Nicole and William having their lunch. She stopped at their table and asked him curiously, 'What is a bacon butty with brown sauce? He asked me to get him one. He is my new boss.' and he told her, 'Just tell them it is for Fred, they know!' After she got that, she stopped at his table one more time and planted a smacker right on his lips and said, 'I got it, you lovely boy!' and zoomed straight out and back into the shop. 'Now that was quick, you will do all right my girl,' Fred remarked. Meanwhile back in the cafe Nicole asked him, 'Who the hell is she?' and he replied smugly, 'That is our new cleaner!' She then stated, 'What is this thing about Indians with you?' and he responded, 'They are hard-working, pleasant people and very nice to look at!' and she remarked, 'I can see some big trouble when Little Stick comes back!'

When she eventually entered that little room upstairs at the end of the day, Jasmine said to herself, "This will do nicely," and dropped her little bundle to the floor. After one quick glance, she reckoned she would need a little help, so she rushed down into the workshop and asked William for some assistance to haul the three mattresses on top of one another. This he gladly did and now he was there, she told him, 'I will need some cleaning products and paint to finish it off!' First thing in the morning, he put his hand in his pocket and took out a ten dollar note saying, 'I reckon that will cover it' and then asked her, 'Is it suitable?' 'More than that, it is almost delightful in this faraway land,' she replied and then she asked him to stay a while longer for a little cuddle. The following morning she arose at six and she leapt out of her bed and rushed downstairs for a quick dust of the furniture and a quick mop of the floor and then went shopping for the things she needed to improve her living space. Fred was well impressed when he came into the shop floor and thought, "now there is a real sweetie, I am glad she is on the books", and both ladies in the shop said, 'there is nothing to do it is as clean as a new pin.' William made no comment but just gleefully smiled. She came back into the shop, with a load of goods and some little plants and two more sweeping brushes with no help from anyone and Nicole remarked, 'Now there is a girl on a mission!' and Roseanne remarked, 'I think she is rather a sweet little thing. I never knew you'd hired a cleaner.'

That evening, Jasmine went to work in her little room and washed down the walls, swept the cobwebs from the ceiling and mopped the floor clean, in that precise order. Then she painted the walls in a brilliant yellow and her door in black and then fixed the broken little table and chair, because they both had wonky legs. She arranged her newly bought little pots of white flowers to give the room a nice fragrance and after all that she flopped into her bed fully dressed. It was nearly midnight but the next morning she awoke at six, fresh as her little plants. Of course they were jasmine just like her name. She popped downstairs into the washroom in the workshop, had a quick wash and brush up and now she was ready for that cleaning job with a little smile on her face.

When the rest of the staff came in they had completely forgotten about her. That didn't apply to William and when he came through that little tunnel he gave her a little peck on the cheek and asked, 'So how did you cope last night?' and she replied, 'All done to my satisfaction.' She added, 'I feel very safe in here,' and he answered, 'Good that you are happy,' and she then responded, 'Very, thanks for that, come up and see me sometime,' to which he replied, 'I will soon.' Now Fred was very pleased with her work and her attention to detail and after about eight weeks he increased her wages to a far more suitable sum. She was delighted with that and gave him a little kiss on his cheek, which was quite a surprise to him and now she was firmly in his favour.

Now, after ten months on the road, Little Stick's band gave up all the small bars and pubs and went on to far bigger venues, which paid a lot more money, because they were getting much more popular. She even started to write some songs for the band, to which they all gave their approval, along with the crowds at their venues. Finally they got a little break from constantly touring and she and Ramona were heading back to their apartment on the train. They both stepped into Little Stick's apartment together and there was Jasmine washing the floor, because now she was contracted to clean the apartments as well and of course she got more money for this. Little Stick barked accusingly at her, 'Who the hell are you?' Jasmine politely responded as she lifted her head said quietly, 'I am the cleaner for this firm,' and added, 'And you are?' But Little Stick didn't reply out of sheer anger. Finding a young pretty girl in her room, she knew straight away who must be totally responsible for it. But young Jasmine didn't even try to explain to this newcomer in the room and she stood her ground firmly. With a final swish on the floor with her mop she left slowly, shutting the door gently behind her, without blinking an eye.

It was three in the afternoon and the only room left to clean was Nicole's. This was a really easy one because she kept her place pretty well. After she had finished she reported to Fred that two strange ladies were in the empty apartment and he remarked, 'So she is back then, don't let her push you around.' She replied defiantly, 'No one pushes me around!' William overheard the conversation and said to her, 'So you have just met Little Stick and Ramona? They are both really nice girls!' and she retorted back to him, 'Maybe to you!' At that point he remembered the jealous streak in her about pretty girls.

Later that evening, after shutting the shop, Jasmine was rushing about wiping down desks and sweeping the floor in her usual swift manner, when all the rest of the staff went into the big room upstairs where they were joined by Little Stick and Ramona. About twenty minutes later Jasmine appeared and she sat right next to William at the big table and brought him a drink from the bar. At the sight of this Little Stick blew her top and asked her straight out, 'Why are you here?' and she responded, 'Sorry I don't explain nor complain, I just do my job. Fred gave me this position to clean the shop and the apartments and he pays me very well, nothing less nor nothing more. So talk to him.' Fred banged the table with his fist and said to Little Stick, 'You are no longer employed here and she is. It was your choice to leave the firm, no one else's, and now you are merely a tenant, so no more of that vile talk to one of my employees otherwise I will cancel your contract here!' Little Stick turned to William and remarked, 'He cannot do that can he?' and he replied, 'Sorry he can, he is the boss hired by Mr Scarlet in London and that is his rule. He paid for the whole setup here and put him in charge not me!' Jasmine just sat there quiet as a mouse with no expression whatsoever throughout the whole scene but she was well aware that she was on unsteady ground. Then Fred banged the table once more and said, 'This meeting is over, the matter is finished, no more ifs or buts!' Little Stick asked Fred, 'Can I have my job back but she has to go?' and he retorted, 'No way, not with that attitude. She stays. I like her work and her way. Talk with me later when you have cooled down!'

So now William had seen a completely new side of her which he thought was well gone when she teamed up with Ramona. He realised that she was deeply attached to him but did he do anything about it? No not really, he just carried on as his normal self. Why? Because he was attracted to pretty brown Indian ladies when he first met them in their camp on the Great Plains and that stuck in his head all this time as they made him feel important. But he never knew why. After all he was just a street lad from smoky old London town, who just wanted to better himself.

The very second that Tim heard that second thump on the table he grinned and left the room because he was headed for his favourite haunt and, not so strangely, he never gave Jasmine a second look because he was only interested in big rounded healthy ladies. Then Ramona gave a tug on Little Stick's arm and took her upstairs to her room, quickly followed by Nicole and both girls gave her their opinion on her future. In the meantime Fred had had enough and he left and went to see his lady friend in town.

Back upstairs Ramona said to Little Stick, 'After all the things you have told me about him, you are out of your mind to just let him go. He is truly the love of your life and that little cleaning girl wouldn't be any threat to you. You now have two choices and they are; one, stay in the band full time or, two, make an effort to get your old job back now. I could easily sing all of your songs myself after all that time we spent on the tour together and you cannot live two lives at the same time.' In came Nicole and she said, 'He brought you here because you asked him, he looked out for you as a young girl without question, he never used you once and he also gave you lots of space to do your own thing again without question!' Little Stick replied, 'I know I know, but it is a hard choice. We have two weeks off. Let me think about it in my own time!' Then Ramona said, 'I think all that adoration you got on that tour went to your head and fumbled your brain and all that bile over finding a girl cleaning your apartment just doesn't make any sense!' She added, 'If it was me I'd jump at the chance to stay with him for life,' and Little Stick then put up her hands and remarked, 'Okay I get the picture. Just let me sleep on it,' and off she went into her bedroom.

So that left just him and Jasmine at the table and he said to her, 'I quite fancy a beer and a walk in the moonlight would you join me?' and she replied, 'I quite like white wine. Is that okay for you?' Off they went walking down the empty streets towards the pub and she slipped her arm through his and he barely noticed because the night was cool and not too dark. He was pretty pleased with Fred's decision on the matter but not too happy with Little Stick's outburst about Jasmine but he still admired her fiery attitude. In the pub they chatted for ages and had quite a few drinks and at the end of the evening he booked a carriage home. That really impressed Jasmine and now she liked him even more than before so she cuddled up real close to him and gave him quite a few kisses in the carriage and he didn't resist because he thought she was a really sweet girl. But now they had a problem to get her back into her room through that little tunnel into the shop and then she suggested to him, 'Look, both of them are out in town so no one will notice if I stay in your apartment because all the girls live upstairs and are probably asleep now so the coast is clear for us!' He wasn't very keen to let this happen but he agreed after a while and said, 'Okay just this once!' and back came the biggest smile he had even seen on a face. She had a plan to make herself totally irresistible and it worked out fairly well for her but he stopped her at the total part, because he had never done it before. At five thirty that morning, she slipped out of his bed softly and kissed his forehead and whispered, 'Thank you for a lovely night,' and then went for a quick shower and brush up. Then she went through the tunnel into the shop and went up into her room to change into her working clothes for the day's chores. When Nicole appeared, she announced, 'Now you look very pleased with yourself this morning,' and she replied sheepishly, 'Well I did keep my position in here thanks to Fred, he is a very fair man,' and Nicole gave a nod of approval back.

William meanwhile still had her on his mind but he shook that off when Fred barked at him, 'Get on with your work boy, no time for daydreaming in here!' He did just that as there was a big order in from Quebec in Canada and it was due out that afternoon on the train. Little Stick was glad to sleep in late that morning in her own bed and then she gave some thought about the events the night before and asked herself, "Was I really that awful to that girl?". Ramona was already wide awake and said to her, 'Roll out of bed now, I am starving hungry. Let's go to the cafe so that I can fill that gap.' Little Stick agreed and bounded out of her bed before she realised that she didn't have to go into the shop anymore as she was now a free woman. But she didn't really feel free now that she was back in her apartment and that feeling had never left her even when she was on tour all that time and why it made her so close to her chosen warrior.

Now she was ready to talk about her future career with someone and she chose Ramona because she had became very close to her on that tour and felt quite relaxed in her company, telling her almost everything in her past. She decided to reveal her plan to her and said, 'I will work in the shop half time and in the band only at local venues because I need to stay close to him just in case!' Ramona retorted, 'I don't think Fred will agree with that. Let's make a new plan. You could continue to write the songs, I will sing them and now and again you could make special appearances in some of the larger venues, maybe at the weekends, so that you wouldn't lose too much time at your job. I think that could just sway him to agreeing and of course there would be no more demanding ways from you!' Little Stick agreed with that in her mind and gave her a nod of her head and told her, 'Okay I will go for that.' Then they finished their third coffee and went back into their apartment for a quick shower and to get ready for a day's shopping in town.

Chapter Fifteen

Down at the shop, in came the telegraph boy with an urgent message and Nicole took it straight upstairs and gave it to Fred. When he opened it, he gave a quick gasp and said to his two colleagues, 'The old man is here in New York with his good lady. He wants someone to pick them up at the station!' Quick as a flash William said, 'I will go.' He stood on the edge of the sidewalk and hailed down a carriage before noticing Jasmine just standing in the doorway with nothing more to do, and he asked her, 'Fancy a ride to the station in a carriage?' She just gave him a silent nod and on the way there, he told her, 'We are going to pick up the big boss all the way from London so be very polite to him. He likes that even more than Fred!' When the couple saw the carriage pull up alongside, Mr Scarlet called over to the man who stepped out of it, 'William is that you?' and he replied, 'It sure is me, welcome to New York, sir!' They shook hands and Mrs Scarlet addressed Jasmine and asked, 'Do you work in the shop also?' and she replied, 'Yes, but I am only a humble cleaner.' She retorted, 'There is nothing humble to cleaning. Someone has to do it. Even me until I met my man, so don't run yourself down like that. Everyone in the world has to do something.' Meantime, Mr Scarlet had a good chat with William and when they arrived at the shop his gaze was fixed on the exterior for quite a while. After a short pause he remarked, 'I truly like what you have done with it.'

Then he went into the shop and all the staff there were trying to shake his hand. 'I don't like all that fuss,' he gruffly remarked and just walked by and spoke to Fred who knew him fairly well and didn't try to attempt it until he addressed him. He said to Fred, 'I would like to see the workshop' and upstairs they went, followed by William and Tim and when he got in there he took a deep breath and stated, 'Clean and fresh, not like your old place I like it!' Fred responded, 'I like to run a tight ship with the help of all of my staff.' Downstairs Mrs Scarlet enjoyed all the fuss she received from the three ladies and then she licked one of her fingers and drew it across one of the desks. She checked it and said to Jasmine, 'Must tell the old man to give you a few more dollars in your pay.' She did just that when he came downstairs and he duly passed it onto Fred.

Then Fred took him into the living quarters for a good look around there and he asked him, 'Do we rent it or did we buy it?' and Fred told him, 'We bought it cheaply because it was a bit rundown and we got a good team to renovate it into its present state. It was not cheap but these premises will go up in price in the future we believe! So it is another asset to the firm.' William then chipped in with, 'This street is in one of the hottest areas in town and the only way is up!' Mr Scarlet then shrewdly asked, 'So what about the turnover?' and Fred stated, 'Very good. This young man increased the sales quite a lot by his trip into the west and his catalogue idea for those out of town clients. He is quite an asset to us here in New York but he does appeal to pretty young ladies.' To which Mr Scarlet remarked, 'There is nothing wrong with that surely. We would all like that!' Then he added, 'He has grown quite a lot from that skinny little kid we took on back home. I barely recognised him at the station with that sweet young Indian girl.'

During this time, Jasmine had been taking Mrs Scarlet for a tour of the living quarters for the staff and she was truly impressed by the whole layout. Then she asked her, 'So which one is yours?' and she replied rather sheepishly, 'Oh I don't live here, my little room is at the top of the shop,' and then she took her up there through the tunnel rather than the main entrance. Mrs Scarlett commented gleefully, 'I just love this secret little tunnel. You could have some clandestine meetings in here!' Now young Jasmine never knew that word but she realised that she had made one big fat mistake going that way, rather than using the front door. She didn't return any comment and took her straight up to her room and in there, the lady remarked, 'You have done it out really nicely but it is a fairly small room.' To which she replied, 'I am a fairly small girl and it's really private and I like it a lot and I never complain. It suits me well!' 'Don't you feel lonely up here?' she asked and Jasmine gave her smile and said, 'Not really. I like a private life, it gives me time to think.' Then they went quietly back downstairs into the shop and Nicole remarked, 'Where did you two spring from I didn't see you come in?' Jasmine whispered to Mrs Scarlet, 'Please don't say a word,' and she didn't.

So who should walk into the shop at that very moment? Why it was only Little Stick after her shopping trip alone, because Ramona had taken all of their bags into their apartment. She was as curious as hell why this little cleaner was chatting to this well-dressed lady in the shop and she asked her outright with blazing eyes, 'Just what is this?' Mrs Scarlet barked back at her, 'So why are you speaking in that manner to one of my staff?' Of course Little Stick didn't know who she was so Nicole put her hands to her face and that gave her a vital clue that she had made one big bloomer. Then William appeared on the scene and told her straight, 'This lady is Mrs Scarlet and this man beside me is Mr Scarlet. They have come all the way from London just to see the shop and we picked them up from the rail station and brought them here. This lady has taken quite a liking to young Jasmine so just cool that hot little head of yours!' Little Stick made no reply.

She left the shop in fury at herself and really slammed the door but luckily for her Nicole saw it coming and eased the pressure on her swing by putting her foot out. She dashed up to her apartment and told Ramona, 'I really blew it this time,' and she remarked, 'It's never over when you still have a chance to repair it,' but she didn't really believe it. Downstairs in the shop, William tried to explain, 'That young lady used to be one of our optometrists and she is very good with kids and old people. She was one very useful member of the firm.' 'Why did she leave?' Mr Scarlett asked him and he explained to him, 'She went on to be a singer in a band. She's very independent and she's still living here in one of our apartments which she is renting at a fair price. Now she wants her position back but that is up to Fred and she has yet to apologise to him because she was quite rude to him at one of our meetings and you know Fred, he is quite against rudeness!' Mrs Scarlet chipped in, 'I quite agree,' and Jasmine just walked away because she didn't want to be involved in shop business.

William then suggested to him, 'Can't you have a word with both of them tonight?' and Mr Scarlet stroked his chin in his usual way and replied, 'Not tonight. Maybe tomorrow just before lunchtime. Let her perspire on it today and Fred I know is a stubborn old goat so he is also cooler in the morning. Make it in here at that time over coffee and the rest of the staff won't be involved, not even you!' and he stated, 'Good, I will arrange it with them.' In came his wife and she simply adored this big room because of the separation between the two floors and she asked him, 'So whose idea was this?' and William replied, 'It was all mine because the two girls needed their private space!' Then the big boss told his wife with pride, 'This is the shoeshine boy from the street who returned my case intact. Didn't he turn out well!' and she responded, 'Indeed,' and added, 'That other little Indian girl, is she any good?' William said, 'She has got that magic charm that makes people very relaxed in her presence,' to which she replied, 'That is not what I saw downstairs today. She came across as a snooty young lady to me.' In her defence he stated, 'She has a real hot temper in some situations, mainly about young ladies close to me!' and she remarked, 'Ah intrigue. I just love a touch of intrigue. So what are you going to do about it?' He cautiously replied, 'Don't really know yet but I'm sure it will work itself out.' Mr Scarlet pushed his chair back and stated, 'Must leave now to go to our hotel, can you hail a carriage for us?' 'Will do,' said William and raced downstairs to call one over and told the driver where to go, gave him some money and off they went.

He delivered the message to both Fed and Little Stick that same night and they both took it quite to their hearts. The next day, Fred sent young Jasmine to their cafe to get his usual along with four coffees and to bring them into the big room. She zoomed off and did just that, because she loved her job. When Mr Scarlet arrived he was more than pleased to see that everything was in order. Then in stepped Little Stick, a little nervous for this meeting, but the big boss put her at ease and asked her, 'Do you really want to keep your position in this firm? If so, you have to apologise to Fred my trusted friend in this business!' She graciously gave him an apology for her rudeness the other night and Mr Scarlet took that as a "yes" and then he asked her for her terms for re-joining the firm. Now this was quite a question to answer and she replied nervously, 'I want to keep my position here but I also want my freedom to perform in my little band – mainly around town but sometimes in bigger venues far away.' Mr Scarlet stated, 'Is that all?' and added, 'You have got it back on full pay but you must inform Fred before you make such a trip long before you take it!' She remarked to him, 'You look far younger than I thought,' and he replied, 'You look far prettier when you smile!' And so the deal was done and she was back on the payroll.

Fred then shook her hand and said, 'Welcome back my little sweetie,' and Mr Scarlet pulled out his gold watch, flipped it open to check the time and told Fred, 'I must fly. My good lady wants to do some shopping and spend my money.' Little Stick dashed quickly upstairs to tell Ramona the good news. She barely got it out but she finally did and said, 'I bloody got it back! I barely said a word but the old gent from England was there and he asked me "what are your terms?". William gave me a glowing report he said, and he took my terms without question and life is great once more thanks to him again!' Ramona stated, 'So it went well? and you wouldn't miss all that touring seven nights a week?' and she retorted, 'No way, I'm back where I belong with my warrior and my apartment and my nice cushy job. What more does a person need?' 'As long as you're happy. I am going to enjoy my final week off,' Ramona replied, 'I'll then be back on the road and I will inform them of your decision to only do the ones that suit you and to let you know if any real big ones come up. So keep writing those tuneful little ditties for me to sing when you are not there.' 'Will do,' replied Little Stick and added, 'Tonight I would like to go out and celebrate my good fortune in a nice little bar.' 'I am up for that,' Ramona agreed, 'I'm going to wear that new suit I've just bought. Why not ask him along too?' to which Little Stick responded, 'You are full of ideas today, why not? I also have a further week off so no big rush in the morning for me. Isn't life wonderful?'

Meanwhile, down in the shop, Mr Scarlet and his wife were back in from their shopping trip and dumped their parcels in there. They were now off to Toronto by train to view another venture for his growing business this side of the pond and he only reappeared to say farewell to his staff. He told Fred, 'Keep in touch more often because the company is growing faster than I imagined!' and he remarked to William, 'I like your taste in young ladies, keep it up. You may soon have another shop here or in Toronto. I'm off to view it today, it's bang smart right in the middle of town!' Then he headed to the waiting carriage and Jasmine kissed him on the cheek as he went out of the main door and he told her with a grin, 'Now you are a real sweetie, hold on to this job for my sake.' She replied, 'I will, you better believe it!' And there was not one tut from Fred who then proclaimed, 'Now that's what I call a businessman. His grandfather would be very proud of him if he was still around!'

Chapter Sixteen

That same evening, Fred went to see his lady in town and Tim went to the house of ill repute to meet a lady companion and Nicole went out to meet her new boyfriend. Both girls entered the middle room and saw William downing a quick beer after a long day and Little Stick asked him straight out, 'Will you join us? We are having a little drink in a bar to celebrate my return to the shop.' 'Just give me some time to change out of my working clothes,' he replied and then he added, 'Can I bring Jasmine along too, because she has also something to celebrate as she's just got a pay rise?' Ramona broke in right there after seeing the look on Little Stick's face and she said, 'Sure, bring her along. It is time to bury the hatchet in the ground!' When he went downstairs, Little Stick rebuked her for that comment but then she realised "tonight I will find the truth". When William got downstairs, he gave Jasmine a call through the tunnel and said, 'We are going out for a little drink tonight in town so put on something smart,' and she called him back, 'I've only got my blue jeans and that checked shirt.' 'That will do nicely,' he replied, but what he didn't tell her was that they weren't going to be on their own. They all met face to face at the main door and that puzzled Little Stick for a while, but she didn't give it much thought at the time.

Now Little Stick's fury had lessened a little by then and she actually spoke to Jasmine in a much lower tone and asked her, 'Where are you from?' Ramona was ready to step in between them, but then realised there was no need for that because they were chatting away quite normally. He was quite relieved at this and said, 'Okay ladies, where will we go? You choose, bar or the pub?' and two of them said the pub. But Little Stick remarked, 'I really miss that little drinking den – shame that we have to give it up. It is where I made my breakthrough into this singing game,' and after a few minutes more in they walked. Of course, it was a brand new band and they were in full flight into a rousing chorus. Nobody took much notice of their arrival and they managed to secure a table in the far corner and the three girls took their seats while he went to the bar to get some drinks. The lady behind there remarked, 'Long time no see,' and he replied, 'Very busy, no time for pleasure,' and she responded, 'I know that feeling,' and back he went with a full tray and everything seemed to be running quite smoothly.

Towards the end of that evening, he excused himself and went to the gents and Little Stick seized her chanced to question Jasmine fully, but she was no fool because she knew this was coming and she repeated everything that he had told her word for word with no hesitation – about the wake in the bar and that she was with the family in there, that she was the cleaner to the old Irish lady and when she died she was out of a job. William had then remarked that his boss was looking for a cleaner who must have good references, which she did, and then he wrote down the address of the shop and gave it to her. That she had gone to to see Fred and he took her on straight away and that was it. Now that all seemed pretty plausible to Ramona and even to Little Stick and then he came back to the table and said, 'Okay girls, time to leave.' Off they went back to their living space, strolling down the dark streets and the girls were laughing and joking all the way there and they headed straight up to the big room for a little more booze. In there Jasmine gave him a little nudge with her hip and said very quietly, 'You took a big chance there!' and he remarked, 'If you have to swim, dive into the deepest part and see what happens!' After a few more drinks, both girls went straight upstairs into their beds and Jasmine then felt a little apprehensive while she was alone with him so close to her apartment and she stated, 'I must go as well. I have a lot to do in the morning. Must get a good night sleep.' Then he went down to his apartment and smiled to himself, with the fact that she really was that cautious not to cause him any trouble.

Now Friday was a busy day for all of them because it was the day to carry out all the odds and ends of the week and they must all be fresh and vigilant at their jobs. That afternoon Jasmine was cleaning out Little Stick's apartment on the top floor. She always gazed out of her big window after she had cleaned it and thought "you can see for miles up here" and then she spotted a familiar sight of those four rough looking men hanging about that little alley just at the end of the street. She said to herself "now that is the third time they have been there at this time of the day, I wonder what they are up to". So she turned to look at the contents of her wardrobe and found Little Stick's bow and a quiver full of arrows wrapped up in an old blanket right in the back. She pulled it out and tried the strength of the pull and thought "now that is one hefty tug". Then she took one of the arrows out, wet her fingers in her mouth then wet the feathers to give it a straighter flight and just let it go straight out of the room and into the wooden beam in the hallway, and remarked to herself, "A fine piece of work, just right for a girl". She pulled the arrow out from the beam and put the lot back where she had found it and carried on with the rest of her cleaning. That was the final apartment done and her working day was now over.

She then went back into the shop through the front door and told Nicole about the four men just outside the little alley and stated, 'That is the third time they have been there. They must be waiting for someone.' Nicole exclaimed, 'Oh my God it's Friday, that is banking day. William always takes the money in the afternoon just after his lunch. They must be after that. He always takes that way because it is a shorter route. It's not a safe way but you know him, he doesn't take any advice from anyone!' Then in he came along with Little Stick and Nicole related all that Jasmine had told her about the men in the alley and he asked her, 'How many?' and she simply replied, 'Too many!' and added, 'Don't give me all that manly guff about you can handle everything.' Now Little Stick enquired, 'What is this all about?' and Nicole remarked, 'He is about to get mugged this afternoon!' 'What are we going to do about it?' Little Stick asked and Jasmine stated, 'You can bring that bow of yours down for a start. I could use it. We could follow him close behind and then when any mischief starts we can go in to help him in a big rush if that is what is needed!' At that point William strolled out of the door with that brown leather bag full of money and he thought it was just a silly little girly game. But they didn't.

Nicole grabbed the broom and got outside to watch his progress towards the alley and then saw the men withdraw baseball bats from under their coats and she shouted loudly, 'Okay girls it is on!' Off they went at speed after the muggers with Little Stick screaming her war cries and hold her skinning knife high above her head. Jasmine stopped in her tracks stood very still, fixed an arrow into the bow and announced, 'Left leg lower muscle,' and then, 'Right arm top shoulder,' and then, 'Left buttock dead middle.' Every one hit right on target and after that the two girls pulled them down fairly easily with help from William who got the other one in a neck grip. Meanwhile Jasmine dutifully retrieved all the spent arrows because she thought they were precious.

After they had all left the shop Roseanne called up to Fred and said to him, 'There is something going on just up the street involving all the girls. I would like you to check it out!' He dashed downstairs and went up to have a look. Seeing everything was under control he walked to the nearby police station and asked for some assistance to remove the culprits and went back to the scene and told William, 'You are one lucky lad.'

Now when Little Stick got the request from Jasmine to bring her bow to her, she trusted her instinct because she was one of them and she also brought her tomahawk and lariat as well just in case, so they could secure the men to something solid like a lamppost. They did just that, so when the police wagon arrived and saw they were all tied up they had no trouble chucking them into the lockup wagon. They asked all of them down to the station to confirm their version of the attack and when they arrived there, the sergeant on the desk remarked, 'It is the Jim Bradley boys, we have been after them for months. There is a reward for them.' Then he asked the group of them who had been involved, 'Which one of you spotted them first?' Everyone pointed to Jasmine and he told her, 'There is fifty dollars waiting in our safe just for you but you will have to sign it out,' and she replied, 'No big problem, I can write in English.' After a few written statements they were free to leave and off they went to the bank but only William and Fred went in and all the girls waited outside. Little Stick remarked, 'Now that was a neat little tumble!' and Jasmine agreed but Nicole admitted she was bloody terrified at first but then she got into the swing of it with her broom alongside the two other girls waving their weapons, screaming at the muggers and Jasmine swiping anyone who got in her way.

Then the two men stepped back outside and they all headed back to the shop and in there Fred handed the three girls a crisp ten dollar note each for their courage, and stated to them, 'Thanks ladies for saving my takings and my good friend William who is one of the best!' They all cheered with gusto at that statement and admiration of the said William and he then gave a short speech to them saying, 'I love you all. Thanks for the back up in the field and for your courage.' And they all replied, 'We love you too!' Fred then took him to one side and murmured to him, 'There is nothing more fearsome than a grateful girl but three of them are even more fearsome. You really are a lucky lad.'

In the meantime Little Stick had a little chat with Jasmine and said, 'You are pretty good with the bow!' and she responded, 'I should be. My skilful grandfather taught me when I was only six years old and he made me practice every day until I hit the middle every time. He was a bowmaker but after the braves got their hands on rifles he didn't get so much work and I thought I must pay him back so I moved to the big city to get him some money. But it wasn't that easy because you needed proper paperwork to get a job here so I took up cleaning work and that is why I ended up here' Little Stick then remarked 'your grandfather was Walking Dog, right, and you are that little kid who won all of the shooting contests with the bow at the age of ten?' Jasmine replied, 'Spot on,' and Little Stick then revealed, 'He made that bow for me. He measured my arm and my pull and made me this, he is a good friend of my dad,' and Jasmine briefly replied, 'Good!' Now Little Stick was growing a touch fonder of her but she still regarded her as a threat because she was a real cutie. But Jasmine was a very cautious girl and she also knew when to keep quiet at times, because she realised that Little Stick didn't really like her. But she could cope with that and she also understood why, because she didn't even know she existed until that day they met in her apartment. She also realised that Little Stick is one really clever cookie – and not because he told her but simply from her manner to other people – and now she grasped the whole picture. But she vowed to carry on her secret meetings with William until that time that he called a halt because she enjoyed his company and he got her the job so she felt it was her loyal duty.

Now on the Saturday following both Little Stick and Ramona went off to Ohio for a big show. It was one of those special ones and she had told Fred well in advance. They left that afternoon to catch the train to Ohio but before she left, she had a little chat to Jasmine and told her straight, 'You can have him while I'm away.' Jasmine retorted with a smile, 'You better tell him that, because he doesn't even know that I exist in that department!' Then she grinned and added, 'Thanks for that, I would love to have him even for a little while!' Now that response really threw Little Stick, and she asked herself, 'Am I really that possessive? Surely not, he does give me lots of room and help to do my own things. Maybe I should just accept him the way he is and give him a little room.' The smile on Jasmine's face became a permanent fixture, but then she cogitated a touch more and was looking for the catch – because there is always a catch. But she couldn't see it and the next meeting for both of them was in the his apartment and this time she brought down some of her little plants just to freshen his room up and then she told him,

'I've got full permission to see you now from her.' Straight away he asked, 'Why?' and she then remarked, 'It is our little secret,' and once again he asked her, 'Why?' Then she went into the shower room and came out smelling just like a Jasmine should and jumped straight into his bed. Now this he couldn't resist and jumped straight in beside her and now she had got him just where she had wanted all along and her sweet aroma just filled up his brain and she could do whatever she could to make him happy.

Little Stick got back into her apartment at seven in the morning, had a little sleep, then knocked on Nicole's door at nine and asked, 'Are you up?' 'I am now,' she replied. After she had let her in, Little Stick revealed to her, 'Last night, big crowd, big money and success,' and she then stated, 'Are you up for a big breakfast?' 'Absolutely,' Nicole replied, 'just let me get dressed,' and down to the cafe they went. In the cafe were William and Jasmine just finishing theirs and Little Stick exclaimed, 'Well well, who do we have here?' Jasmine's guard was up straight away and he said a polite, 'Good morning,' to her but that wasn't enough for her and she nearly made a scene. But Nicole requested to her, 'Just calm down and take a seat,' and he asked her, 'Was it a good show?' but she refused to answer him and just grunted a little and Nicole remarked, 'You are just a silly girl.' Out went William quickly followed by Jasmine to take a little walk in the sunshine.

Jasmine then said to him, 'You once again took a big risk going there don't you think so?' and he replied, 'We are merely friends having some breakfast together, relax.' But she inquired, 'So how did I get out of a locked shop to meet you? I've got no key to have done that?' He just scoffed at that remark and stated, 'But I do!' That was not the end of it however because Little Stick paid him a visit at his place to asked him out to lunch. Of course Jasmine was well gone at that time but when she stepped in, she got of whiff of jasmine straight away from that little plant she brought down to him. But she said not a word to him about it, and then asked him, 'How about a little lunch on me we had a great show last night and some big bucks!' That put him off his guard because he was expecting a blinding argument after this morning, and he took that as an all clear. She went back to his place for a little cuddle and a bit more. And he did just that to her immense joy with all that new touching and feeling the exact places she wanted him to and that was all new to her. Now she was almost certain that he had been regularly practising on someone, because when she first met him he was a shy young man barely able to give her a cuddle on a cold night in the Great Plains. But now she was pretty happy with his new-found approach to her and that gave her some new thoughts. Her clever little brain had now worked it out that they had been together for quite a time and he developed into a quite pleasing fresh young gentleman. But she wasn't displeased with that. And why? Because now he was ready to try anything she suggested to him and she gave him plenty of space to do so, because it made him more amorous towards her and it brightened up their relationship when they were together.

So Little Stick eventually let them meet up freely without any comment because she had reckoned that Jasmine had done her a good turn through teaching him a more hands-on approach towards girls. After some time she even invited her out for a meal with them which brought Jasmine's guard right up, because now she knew that Little Stick knew and that made her even more cautious in her company. William was pretty pleased as he was in the company of two lovely girls at the same time and they now became friendly. But that was only the vision that he chose to see.

Before Little Stick's next big gig in Pittsburgh on a Saturday evening and when they were putting away everything on the Friday evening just before lock up, she asked Jasmine pleasantly, 'I would love to see your little room upstairs?' and she bluntly retorted, 'Why?' She replied, 'I am just curious,' and Jasmine then knew in her head that something was at the back of this request and she simply refused to do so. But Little Stick wasn't one to just give up and she followed her up there and when Jasmine opened her door out came that aroma of jasmine and in she stepped and said to herself, "Now it is proven!" She stated laconically, 'Listen cutie I can smell your presence on him. That is my man so just back off and find someone else!' Jasmine knew that tone well and replied, 'I have nothing to explain, we are merely friends,' to which she retorted, 'Just don't get too friendly with him!' Jasmine did not reply to that but then stated, 'You do know they lock the door after they put up the grills so you really have to leave now!' Little Stick uttered, 'Holy shit I had forgotten about that!' Then she raced downstairs just in time but Fred was already outside ready to lock up, so she rapped on the door and said, 'Let me out Fred!' He of course didn't know she was in there and asked her, 'So where have you been?' and she replied, 'Just upstairs having a little chat with Jasmine.' 'Any trouble?!' he enquired and she answered, 'Not at all, just running through a few things with her' and he took that as gospel.

She went straight up to her apartment and thought it over. She didn't have the nerve to asked William straight out at that time, even though he appeared up at her place and said, 'Fancy a little drink tonight in a bar?' She almost gulped out her reply and said, 'Just let me change into something more suitable.' Then off they went to a quiet little place not too far away and now she had a lot more nerve, and remarked to him, 'When you were teaching me on your guitar you always told me practice makes perfection.' 'Very true,' he replied, 'so what?' Now she revealed to him somewhat reluctantly, 'All that time I was on the road I improved myself on the guitar with a little help from my fellow guitarist and without her input I would have remained at the level you taught me.' Just then she gave a little thought about what she was about to reveal and realised that if she stated it, it would put him in a mood and it would also cause great animosity between them and also Fred would need to sack Jasmine and he would get a bit grumpy towards her too. So she quickly changed the subject and he said, 'Well what is your point?' and she replied, 'Oh it's not important,' and off they went back home holding hands.

Now Saturday was a busy day because that was when all the children came in to see the Indian lady because she was so nice. Fred told her, 'You are in charge of all those unruly little pests!' but she didn't mind, although of course she had to catch an early train to Pittsburgh for that big event tonight. That same night, William took Jasmine into town for a nice meal then back to his place for a little cuddle and she stayed overnight but she never mentioned the visit last night from her. Little Stick came back from her gig in Pittsburgh at seven thirty in the morning and the band wagon dropped her off at the shop as usual. On the way home, she had a little sleep on the train but she still needed some more so she went straight to bed. About nine, Nicole rapped on her door and called, 'Wakey wakey little star, time for brekkies,' and out she sprang and opened her door. She said to her, 'What a night. They all sang "hit us with your songs Little Stick" when we came on for the second half and they wouldn't stop until I started. It is one of those big concert halls which echoes every sound and there were nearly one thousand people in there and I'm really glad I don't do that every night, my little job here suits me real fine!' Then in they went to the cafe and right behind them were Jasmine and William.

Jasmine sat down at the same table as Little Stick while he and Nicole ordered their choices at the counter and Jasmine said to her, 'I come in peace!' and she replied, 'I said nothing to him,' and Jasmine then revealed, 'Me neither!' So both of them were happy with the outcome as it was. All four of them went for a leisurely stroll in the park after their breakfast and he walked with Nicole and the other two were far in front of them, talking naturally like old friends. He remarked to her, 'I will never understand girls,' and she replied, 'We are a strange lot and that goes for me too.' Up front Little Stick told Jasmine, 'I used my discretion!' who retorted, 'I only used my common sense because the result if that came out would be that I would lose my job and you would probably lose yours and your apartment. So now friends for ever!' and then they slapped hands like a couple of school kids and that little stroll took longer than they expected because they walked around the park three times. William and Nicole were simply amazed by their behaviour but they still stayed well back from them. By now it was almost lunchtime and he reckoned it was a good idea to take all of them for a swish lunch up town and of course they were all up for that because he was paying for it. When they sat down in this posh restaurant Jasmine ordered white wine all around and now Little Stick was further convinced that he was taking her out, but now she was not so displeased because she was one of them. William then took the waiter's arm and told him, 'Just a cold beer for me.' After they got back home, he opened the shop's door to let Jasmine in up to her room and then Little Stick invited him up to her place and remarked, 'She is quite a pleasant young girl, very pretty don't you think so?' He quickly responded, 'Not as pretty as you are!' and then she asked him, 'Are you still my warrior?' and he replied,

'Nothing has changed between me and you!' That put a big smile on her face and she asked him, 'Stay awhile with me. I need a little reassurance that you still desire me,' and his reply was, 'No question about it, you are my true Cherokee princess!' and then he gave her a big tight hug.

She kept him a while longer in her room than that, because all that fiery hot streak in her had simply disappeared and had turned into passion just because of that compromise she had made with Jasmine which was, 'Don't tell a soul, not even him.' After he left that evening she picked up her guitar and gave it a little strum and thought "now that would make a great song and would apply to quite a lot of people". Then she scribbled down a few words and went to bed humming the words of Keep It To Yourself with a big smile on her pretty face. And up she sprang on Monday morning fresh as a daisy, ready for a good day's work and gave Jasmine a cheery good morning while she was wiping her desk down. Jasmine returned her greeting also with a smile and Nicole remarked to her, 'What did you have last night? I need to have some of the same,' and Little Stick quietly responded, 'I have found a new approach to my life.' She had a little scar just above her top lip on the left side of her face and she thought it was quite unattractive but he did not even notice it nor comment on it and to her, that was the perfect warrior.

Mutt the Dog

───※───

Mutt the dog was in Alaska living in the wilds near the goldfields and early one morning he was caught in a trap by his left lower leg. He howled loudly at his pain and along came a grizzled old gold prospector heading to his claim, swigging from his whisky bottle which was his only breakfast, who heard the howls. He set off in that direction and found that poor animal and he snapped open the trap. The wolf snapped at him twice and he said to it, 'Listen Mutt, I would like to help you to recover, you silly Mutt.' So he skipped the trip to his claim that morning and took the animal back to his little cabin, which he had built himself log by log. It was no palace but he did have the basics to repair a wound; a little alcohol and a few well-chosen leaves and some selected mud to seal his leg, so that it could heal properly. After a few days he was walking on it but the old man kept him in his cabin for some time because he knew he was not quite up to scratch so he left him in there while he went to find his fortune in the fields.

Mutt was quite happy with this old man's presence because he fed him well and he even talked to him in the evening. Then when his claim ran out and he had accrued enough gold to buy a little plot in the big city, he upped sticks and headed to New York. He found a nice little piece of land just behind a police station and now he was ready for a brand new trade – transporting criminals to the jailhouse from the streets. He was pretty good at it with the help of his fearsome dog but sadly he passed away at the grand old age of seventy-seven and that is when William spotted the wagon outside the police station.

His name was Zeb Zablinski. He was from Russia and had been living in Siberia so he didn't have too far to travel to the goldfield in Alaska. He went there to improve his life, just like many others after him. He didn't make a great fortune but just enough to settle down in the big city on his own terms and he was quite content with that. This was long before the great gold rush in Alaska, which was the given name after America bought it from Russia just after he moved there, but did he care? Not in the least. He just wanted to have a better life in this new continent, whatever it threw in his direction.

Lightning Source UK Ltd.
Milton Keynes UK
UKHW010836190223
417246UK00004B/140